Evald Flisar

Alice in Crazyland

Translated from the Slovene by
Andrej Pleterski

Texture Press
NORMAN, OKLAHOMA
2015

EVALD FLISAR (1945, Slovenia). Novelist, playwright, essayist, editor, globe-trotter (travelled in 96 countries), underground train driver in Sydney, editor of (among other publications) an encyclopaedia of science and invention in London, author of short stories and radio plays for the BBC, president of the Slovene Writers' Association (1995 – 2002), since 1998 editor of the oldest Slovenian literary journal Sodobnost (Contemporary Review), since April 2015 President of the Slovene PEN Center. Author of 13 novels (nine of them short-listed for kresnik, the Slovenian "Booker"), two collections of short stories, three travelogues, two books for children, and fifteen stage plays (eight nominated for Best Play of the Year Award, three times won the award). Winner of the Prešeren Foundation Prize, the highest state award for prose and drama and the prestigious Župančič Award for lifetime achievement. Various works translated into 36 languages, among them Bengali, Hindi, Malay, Nepalese, Indonesian, Turkish, Greek, Japanese, Chinese, Arabic, Czech, Albanian, Lithuanian, Icelandic, Romanian, Amharic, Russian, English, German, Italian, Polish, Spanish, etc. His stage plays are regularly performed all over the world, most recently in Austria, Egypt, India (three different productions in two months alone), Indonesia, Japan, Taiwan, Serbia, Bosnia, Bulgaria, Belarus and USA. Attended more than 50 literary readings and festivals on all continents. Lived abroad for 20 years (three years in Australia, 17 years in London). Since 1990, resident in Ljubljana, Slovenia. His novel My Father's Dreams, published by Texture Press in 2005 and recently by Istros Books in London, UK, has earned him a place at the European Literature Night, an annual event at the British Library that features 6 of the best contemporary European writers. Another of his novels, On the Gold Coast (published in English by Sampark, Kolkata, India) was nominated for the most prestigious European literary prize, the Dublin IMPAC International Literary Award. It was listed by The Irish Times as one of 13 best novels about Africa written by Europeans, alongside Joseph Conrad, Graham Greene, Isak Dinesen, JG Ballard, Bruce Chatwin and other great literary names. In June/July 2015 the author completed a three-week literary tour of USA, reading at the Congress Library in Washington and SUA convention in Chicago, attending the performance of his play Antigone Now at the Atlas Performing Arts Center in Washington, speaking at the Slovenian Permanent Mission at the United Nations, etc.

*t*P

Texture Press

Evald Flisar

Alice in Crazyland

Translated from the Slovene by
Andrej Pleterski

Texture Press
NORMAN, OKLAHOMA
2015

Evald Flisar, ALICE IN CRAZYLAND
Copyright © Evald Flisar

Translation copyright © Andrej Pleterski
Andrej Pleterski has received a grant from the Slovenian Book Agency.

Originally published in Slovenia (European Union) as *Alica v nori deželi*
(Ljubljana: Vodnikova založba & Sodobnost International, 2010.)

Published in the United States by
Texture Press, 1108 Westbrooke Terrace, Norman, OK 73072

Editor
Susan Smith Nash, PhD

Sub-editor
Arlene Ang

Cover design
Pšena Kovačič and Arlene Ang

Published with the financial assistance of Trubar Foundation, Ljubljana, Slovenia.

ISBN 978-0692561737 (Texture Press)

For performance rights please contact sodobnost@guest.arnes.si.

Printed in the United States of America.

Texture Press
Norman, OK 73072
USA
texturepress@beyondutopia.com

ALICE
IN
CRAZYLAND

Characters:

Alice
Professor Jumper
Potter Potts
Pottsy-Wottsy
Pottpot
Potteroonko
Potterola
Potterspot
Pottiela
Blue Officer
Red Officer

ACT 1

Scene One

The Triglav Lakes Valley. Alice runs into a funny apparition sitting on the floor, its back resting against a rucksack, eyes closed. Alice tries to tiptoe past it.

PROFESSOR: Alice!

ALICE: *(Surprised.)* Uncle! What are you doing here?

PROFESSSOR: *(Shaking his bald head.)* Resting. And why are you not at school?

ALICE: I have degrees from three faculties. I'm a researcher now.

PROFESSOR: At the age of twelve? Researching what?

ALICE: The rubbish we believe in without asking ourselves whether it's true.

PROFESSOR: Such as …

ALICE: Why do we still believe it was Christopher Columbus who discovered America, although we've known for some time it was Leif Eriksson?

PROFESSOR: Really? *(Stands up.)* You've grown a hell of a lot since we last saw each other. *(Stands on his toes.)* Now I'm going to jump into the lake down there. To freshen up for a long journey.

ALICE: To the top of Mt Triglav?

PROFESSOR: *(In confidence.)* I'm off to an island country in the Caribbean, Trinidad and Tobago.

ALICE: On holiday?

PROFESSOR: No, their economy has fallen to pieces. They've hired me to help them set it right.

ALICE: I didn't know the world still considered you an expert.

PROFESSOR: *(Takes a breath and starts packing his rucksack.)* If you hadn't made fun of me, I'd take you along. But you're still a child. You'd be more of a hindrance than help. I'm too old for such things, so I'm going alone.

ALICE: Have a safe trip.

PROFESSOR: Right after an invigorating swim in that pond over there.

ALICE: That's not a pond, Uncle, it's one of Triglav Lakes!

PROFESSOR: Water is water. The only problem is I don't feel like walking there. I'll just jump.

ALICE: Isn't it too far?

PROFESSOR: Have you forgotten we practiced jumping into the air when you were still a kid?

ALICE: No, I haven't.

PROFESSOR: We could jump effortlessly hand in hand from Congress Square to Ljubljana Castle and from the Castle to Rožnik Hill. Not something you can forget.

(He makes two steps backwards to take a run.)

ALICE: You're forgetting you can't swim, Uncle!

(PROFESSOR JUMPER, however, has already bounced off the ground and is whizzing like a cannonball across the clearing and the spruces towards the surface of the lake. ALICE takes a deep breath.)

Oh, God! Now what?

(Takes a run and goes flying after PROFESSOR JUMPER. We hear some horrendous roaring, breaking, slamming, splashing. Then silence... When the lights come on, ALICE is lying soaked to the skin, along with her rucksack, on a sandy beach at the seaside. Sprawled on the sand, not far away and no less soaked, is PROFESSOR JUMPER, along with his rucksack.)

Uncle! I've never been happier to see you!

PROFESSOR: *(Sitting upright.)* What happened?

ALICE: We were travelling to Trinidad and Tobago. Then a tsunami caught up with us, triggered by a submarine earthquake. It flung the ship high in the air as though it were no heavier than a box of matches.

PROFESSOR: Impossible.

ALICE: Then it sank. Together with the passengers. Except for you and me. We were deposited on this desert island.

PROFESSOR: I'm not used to swearing, but at this very moment … holy smoke, I bloody well wish I was!

ALICE: Goodness, Uncle! How come you can't remember the tsunami? You must have sustained a concussion!

PROFESSOR: Quite the contrary! It's you who sustained a concussion. I can't remember anything because nothing happened, while you're imagining things.

(He stands up and starts to rinse his shirt; water is dripping from it.)

ALICE: Why are we wet then?

PROFESSOR: We may have stumbled and fell. Into a puddle. Or a pond. There are countless options.

ALICE: Except for the most obvious one – that we were swept ashore by a tsunami.

PROFESSOR: If this were so, we wouldn't be soaked like a pair of cats that fell asleep in a dishwasher. Sharks would be playing tennis with us at the bottom of the ocean instead!

(He spreads the rinsed shirt on the sand and sits down. ALICE walks up to him, takes his head in her hands and shakes it vigorously.)

ALICE: I read somewhere that a concussion can be neutralized by twisting the head in the opposite direction. *(Shakes his head firmly again.)*

PROFESSOR: Stop shaking my head as if you were trying to behead me.

ALICE: It obviously works! Let's see if you can remember anything now. We were on the ship, sailing to Trinidad and Tobago, standing on the deck, gazing across the sea …

PROFESSOR: And you said, what did you say?

ALICE: No, it was you who said it. Alice, you said, for some time I have been gathering courage to make you an offer.

PROFESSOR: What offer?

ALICE: To become your assistant!

PROFESSOR: Which doesn't change the fact that you must obey every word I say. If not every single one, at least every second one. Or the third one!

ALICE: Have you forgotten I accepted your proposal on one condition? *(PROFESSOR gives her a puzzled look.)* To be always friendly and kind to me? And to let me play a trick or two on you from time to time?

PROFESOR: Shouldn't we rather be asking ourselves where the hell we are?

ALICE: You're right.

PROFESSOR: *(Makes a few steps, folds his arms on his back and raises his head as if looking far across the sea.)* We're standing on the beach of the island of Trinidad and Tobago.

ALICE: Are you sure?

PROFESSOR: We've reached our destination, Alice! We just need to look for the nearest way to the capital.

ALICE: Uncle?

PROFESSOR: Yes?

ALICE: Trinidad and Tobago are two tropical islands with lush greenery. Look around. Not even a blade of grass anywhere.

PROFESSOR: *(Looks around.)* That's fine! Beyond the horizon, palm trees will start swinging above our heads, and we shall inhale the sweet smells of pineapples and oranges. *(Puts on his shirt.)*

ALICE: I doubt it very much.

POTTS: So do I.

(PROFESSOR JUMPER and ALICE almost jump out of their skin, stiffening for five seconds. Then they turn around.)

PROFESSOR and ALICE: Oh my!

Scene Two

Not far from them stands a man dressed in grey with a grey briefcase and grey clogs on his feet, thin as though he has been starving for the whole year.

ALICE: Who are you?

POTTS: Who are *you*? *(Looks at PROFESSOR.)* And who are you, sir?

PROFESSOR: *(Straightening up.)* Professor Jumper from Slovenia, a world-famous expert making regular appearances on TV. Your government has hired me to fix your economy because you will soon have nothing to eat. Looking at you, I can see the situation is even worse than I thought. But never mind, you're obviously a member of the Official Reception Committee.

(The grey man walks around PROFESSOR as if trying to take a closer look at him. Then he walks around ALICE, who seems to have made a slightly better impression on him.)

POTTS: No, sir, I'm the head of the department that issues entrance permits to foreigners who are washed ashore on our beaches. *(Opens his grey briefcase, takes out a bunch of forms and offers them to PROFESSOR.)* Fill out these ten forms and sign each of them twenty-one times. In your own handwriting.

PROFESSOR: *(Takes the sheets of paper.)* On one condition. If I can fill them out in Japanese and sign each of them five hundred times in somebody else's handwriting.

ALICE: *(Showing moral support by clapping her hands.)* Well done, Uncle!

POTTS: Under such condition, you are subject to the rule of filling out the forms with three pens at once and signing them by writing your name and surname simultaneously with both the capital and the small letters.

PROFESSOR: Who made up such rules?

POTTS: The Committee for Making Up Stupid Rules, who else?

PROFESSOR: Alice, a while earlier you claimed to be my assistant, say something!

ALICE: Uncle, this friendly gentleman is only trying to tell us the people of Trinidad and Tobago have a sense a humour.

POTTS: Trinidad and Tobago? What's that?

PROFESSOR: That, for goodness' sake, is the country where we're standing!

POTTS: The name of this country, sir, is Potteroonia.

ALICE: *(Takes a deep breath.)* Potteroonia?

PROFESSOR: Listen, man. In broad daylight, while on duty, you're drunk as a skunk. I'll have to report this to the authorities. What's your name?

POTTS: *(Kindly.)* My name is Potts, sir. I have to vaccinate you against potti fever. I'm in charge of the National Health Service. *(He takes a huuuuuge syringe out of his briefcase, larger than anything ALICE and PROFESSOR have ever seen in their lives.)* The syringe is a bit long, but we had to make

16

it longer because we discovered that some people have very thick skin. Close your eyes and bend over.
PROFESSOR: I have back problems …

(With a sudden movement, POTTS removes PRO-FESSOR's glasses, dropping them at his feet. PRO-FESSOR leans forward to pick them up but can't see them. ALICE leans forward as well, to pick up the glasses. With both of them bent over, POTTS jabs the long needle into their bottoms, first PRO-FESSOR's and then ALICE's.)

ALICE: Aaargh!
PROFESSOR and ALICE: *(In unison.)* Eeeyouch!
POTTS: *(Puts the injection away in his briefcase.)* We're done with this, now hand over your luggage.
PROFESSOR: *(Puts his glasses on.)* You must have fled from the nuttiest nuthouse in the world! I cannot express my disappointment with your behaviour other than by telling you straight in the face that I'm speechless!
POTTS: Excellent!

(He drags both rucksacks across the grey plateau into the island's hinterland until the only thing remaining is a grey spot in the distance. Brief silence.)

ALICE: What do you suggest, Uncle?
POTTS: We should take advantage of the man's absence and run.

ALICA: Back to the sea or inland?

PROFESSOR: To find the police! To report this shameless theft!

ALICE: There was nothing special in my rucksack, just a cheese sandwich.

PROFESSOR: Do you know what was in mine? The manuscript of my latest book, *How to Solve Economic Problems of the World by a Single Stroke*!

ALICE: You can write it again.

PROFESSOR: I've been writing it for five years!

POTTSY-WOTTSY: Good afternoon.

(PROFESSOR and ALICE slowly turn around and find a rather obese gentleman in police uniform standing before them, grinning stupidly. He also seems to have rolled around in ashes for days.)

PROFESSOR: The police?

POTTSY-WOTTSY: How can I help you?

PROFESSOR: Some runaway fool has duped us with some far-fetched story ...

POTTSY-WOTTSY: Just a moment, sir. Your watch, please. *(PROFESSOR, as though hypnotized, hands him his watch.)* And yours, miss. *(ALICE also hands him her watch as though hypnotized.)* And your bracelet. And your necklace. And your hairpin, miss. And all your rings. *(ALICE hands everything to the friendly police officer as if doing the most natural thing in the world.)* Thank you. Goodbye.

18

(POTTSY-WOTTSY *stuffs all the collected items into the pockets of his jacket, turns around and rushes inland across the sandy plateau.*)

PROFESSOR and ALICE: *(Waving politely.)* Good-bye …

(Then they stop, gazing at the ground before them, without daring to look at each other.)

ALICE: Uncle, don't you feel we've done something stupid?
PROFESSOR: Why? The policeman suspected the dangerous deceiver was still nearby, so he decided to deposit our valuables somewhere safe.
ALICE: Kick me, I might wake up.
PROFESSOR: I don't know about kicking, but I heard that one can be brought back to reality by a good slap.

(ALICE and PROFESSOR JUMPER start slapping each other. The sounds reverberate along the beach – smack, smack, snap, crack bang, slam, boom.)

ALICE: Are you awake?
PROFESSOR: Not quite. But I'm grossly swollen. Why did you hit me so hard?
ALICE: To wake you up in case this was a dream.
PROFESSOR: Obviously it isn't. We'll have to follow developments.

19

POTTS: Good idea.

(Alice and Professor jump up and turn around. The grey malnourished rogue who stole their luggage stands before them. He offers them some sort of clogs: the smaller pair for ALICE and the bigger one for PROFESSOR.)

PROFESSOR: What's this?
POTTS: Shoes, sir. And yours, miss.
PROFESSOR: There must be some mistake.
POTTS: There is no mistake.

(He places the bigger pair of clogs at PROFESSOR's feet. Then he straightens up and slaps him.)

ALICE: Oh, dear! I also think it's not a mistake.
PROFESSOR: Listen, you! A policeman just took a precious watch from me, and even more precious jewellery from my niece. And you're offering me some sort of … what are these clogs made of, anyway?
POTTS: Potti, sir. *(Gives PROFESSOR another slap.)*
PROFESSOR: Potti? Alice, what is that?
POTTS: I believe it's a … Ah, I see … That's for sure … Or maybe not … It's a … Anyway, why don't you ask this respectful gentleman?
PROFESSOR: Sir … *(POTTS gives him another slap.)* Why are you slapping me all the time?

20

POTTS: Just a second. An informative lecture is coming up. *(He steps a little to the side, pulls a small clay tablet from his pocket, blows some dust from it, straightens up and starts to read.)* In most countries, consumer and productive goods are made of steel. Aluminium. Concrete. Wool. Animal skin. Wood. Materials that no longer exist in Potteroonia. However, we do have potti. It's actually the only thing we've got left. Which means it's forbidden to bring to Potteroonia anything that's not made of potti. Except for exceptions. The few things that can't be made of potti. Such things, however, do not exist. *(He pushes the tablet back into his pocket.)* Did you understand the lecture?

PROFESSOR: And who was the lecturer?

POTTS: Professor Potter Potts, the Authorized Informant for Uninformed Aliens.

PROFESSOR: Can Professor Potts inform us what happened to our valuables?

POTTS: They've become potti stew! Pottsy-Wottsy has minced them!

ALICE: Pottsy-Wottsy?

POTTS: Who else? Pottsy-Wottsy, a Customs Decomposer of Accidentally Imported Undesired and Extremely Harmful Substances and Items. Your shoes will meet a similar fate once you finally decide to take them off and put on these potti sandals. The sooner, the better!

(ALICE and PROFESSOR remove their shoes without further objection and hand them to POTTS. The latter squeezes them under his armpit and heads for the grey inland.)

PROFESSOR: *(Shouting after him.)* Where are you going?

POTTS: *(From a distance.)* To arrange your transport!

(Brief silence.)

PROFESSOR: Alice, on which coast would we land if we jumped in the air right now and fly across the sea?

ALICE: I think we would end up right in the middle of the ocean, Uncle. *(Puts on potti clogs and makes a few awkward steps; they creak awfully.)* At least we've got something, haven't we?

Scene Three

We can hear peculiar roaring, as though an excavator, a dustbin lorry, a racing car and a juddering washing machine were moving along together. A strange vehicle appears. Looking at it, it is almost impossible to decide whether it reminds one more of a boat or a car or rather an abortive combination of both, if not something else. Or something completely different. The only thing certain is that POTTER

POTTS *is sitting behind the wheel, and beside him sits the pudgy gentleman in police uniform, whose name is supposed to be* POTTSY-WOTTSY.

POTTS: A taxi for you, sir.
POTTSY-WOTTSY: And for you, miss.
PROFESSOR: Where's Mr Taxi Driver taking us?
POTS: Around the corner and joyfully forwards, as they say.
POTTSY-WOTTSY: Joyfully forwards! *(He claps like a child looking forward to a trip to the seaside.)*
ALICE: My goodness, how can you put up with this noise? My eardrums are about to burst!
POTTSY-WOTTSY: There is no point in that. If ears were made of potti, I'd have at least a small benefit from the shards, but since they're not, you'd better keep them where God decided they should be. Ha-ha! Haha!
PROFESSOR: Not to mention what noise there must be on motorways! A normal human being can't possibly survive that without earplugs.
POTTS: Sir! You've given me a marvellous idea for a new potti product! Potti earplugs! I can see you're a first-class inventor. *(Whispering in* PROFESSOR*'s ear.)* We must reach a private agreement. To a substantial benefit for both of us, I have no doubt.
PROFESSOR: Neither do I. *(Gives* POTTS *a slap.)* However, it all depends on which one of us is faster in teaching the other about the basic rules of polite behaviour.

POTTS: I agree. (*Slaps* PROFESSOR *back.*) And now I kindly ask both of you to take a seat in the taxi.

POTTSY-WOTTSY: One, two, three!

PROFESSOR: Alice, as my assistant, what do you suggest?

ALICE: (*Settles herself in one of the backseats of the vehicle.*) As the gentleman put it: around the corner and joyfully forwards.

POTTSY-WOTSY: Joyfully forwards!

(The vehicle moves forwards and takes a circular path around the stage.)

PROFESSOR: What is this clattercar called?

POTTS: Pottiyota Mark 2 Super 16V.

PROFESSOR: Are there many traffic accidents in your country?

POTTS: Far fewer than provided for by the national plan. A serious problem, but we're doing our best to improve the situation.

(The vehicle drives offstage. A horrendous blast, the sound of something being crushed, some clattering. The following conversation takes place offstage.)

PROFESSOR: Oh, dear! My glasses!

ALICE: Here you are, Uncle! Are you all right?

PROFESSOR: No. There is a big gaping hole in my head.

ALICE: Where?

PROFESSOR: Here!

ALICE: That is your mouth!

PROFESSOR: It's never been so big!

ALICE: Keep it shut and it'll become smaller. We have a bigger problem: the driver and Pottsy-Wottsy have disappeared.

PROFESSOR: Hardly a problem. We could have struck a deal with the former, but the latter, excuse my French, is an imbecile.

(He and ALICE crawl back onstage on all fours.)

ALICE: Maybe so, but he seems quite a likeable fellow. He reminds me of the two gentlemen I met in the country behind the looking glass. The name of the former was Tweedledee and the other was Tweedledum.

PROFESSOR: Oh! Here they are!

(POTTS and POTTSY-WOTTSY crawl back onstage on all fours.)

POTTS: I can't remember the last time I was so pleased with myself! Both cars gone! A very successful day.

PROFESSOR: And who caused the accident?

POTTS: Me, who else! You're my witness.

PROFESSOR: But …

POTTS: You saw very well that I moved to the other side of the road on purpose. Surely you aren't walking out on me now, after all I've done for you?

POTTSY-WOTTSY: Surely not!

PROFESSOR: What about the rest of the road, are we going to walk?

POTTS: Are you joking? The police are already on their way. Bringing me a replacement vehicle.

POTTSY-WOTTSY: And the certificate!

POTTS: And the certificate proving I've done good work for the community.

PROFESSOR: Can you give me another slap, Alice? I might be dreaming, after all.

ALICE: You'd better give one to me, Uncle.

POTTS: Let me help you. *(Slaps* PROFESSOR, *then* ALICE.*)* Still dreaming?

Blackout.

Scene Four

When the lights turn on, our heroes enter a grey room.

PROFESSOR: Where are we?

POTTS: You've come to my place for tea.

(Beckons to POTTSY-WOTTSY, *who instantly places a potti table and three potti chairs in the middle of the room. Then he disappears through the door into the adjacent room.)*

PROFESSOR: What did you say was the name of the capital city?

POTTS: Pottington.

PROFESSOR: Everything is made of potti. Buildings, pavements, streets, traffic signs, clattercars. Even litter bins.

POTTS: Yes.

PROFESSOR: Why do people keep throwing their chairs, tables, cupboards and pots through the windows with such enthusiasm? And why is everything shattered to smithereens as if made of potti?

POTTS: Because it *is* made of potti.

ALICE: *(Looking out the window.)* Even the trees.

POTTS: My idea – if I may boast a bit. After the last wooden trees disappeared we agreed to install replacements. As a result, all our trees are very original –produced by renowned artists, from the first to the very last one.

(Suddenly, the floor starts to rock. PROFESSOR JUMPER *stretches his arms to hold on to something,* ALICE *also flaps her arms.* POTTER POTTS *strides around casually. We can hear a hollow rumble.)*

PROFESSOR: An earthquake?

POTTS: That's what we used to call it. But not any more. It's simply wind blowing through the caves of the potti mine under the city.

PROFESSOR: *(Horrified.)* You dig potti from under the city?

POTTS: We have exhausted all other locations.

PROFESSOR: Oh my God!

ALICE: Are you trying to say that the city can crash into the cave under our feet?

POTTS: Of course. This can happen at any moment. But since nobody knows when it will happen, we've learned to live believing that it will happen eventually, but never at *this* particular moment.

PROFESSOR: Thank you for your concise clarification of Potteroonian logic.

ALICE: Oh dear! Uncle, how could we have forgotten that the government of Trinidad and Tobago is waiting for us? You signed a contract, remember?

PROFESSOR: *(Pointing out the window.)* Why are they removing that big statue?

POTTS: Because statues of great men in history are being gradually relocated underground to support the weakening crust under the city. This way great men can continue to play their historic roles even after death.

PROFESSOR: But surely there can't be that many great men in history.

POTTS: Indeed. That's why a few months ago we stopped cremating corpses. Now we embalm them, drive them into subterranean caves and stack them into support pillars.

PROFESSOR: And so even ordinary citizens can be exemplary pillars of society after death.

POTTS: What more could one wish for?

PROFESSOR: But still …

(POTTSY-WOTTSY *brings three potti cups and a potti teapot. He puts them on a potti coffee table, takes a bow and curves his mouth into an obliging smile.*)

POTTS: We take advantage of shards, too. Recycling has reached its climax here.

ALICE: Uncle, may I have an urgent word with you in private? *(Stamps her feet impatiently and swings her arm. She sweeps one of the potti cups off the table. The cup falls on the floor and shatters.)* Oh, I'm so sorry.

POTTS: Pottsy, the form. (POTTSY-WOTTSY *instantly pulls a piece of brownish paper and a pencil out of his pocket, handing both to* ALICE.) Write down the date and briefly describe the processed object, miss. Do this every time you recycle something. The forms are collected at the end of each month. *(Turns to* POTTSY.) Give a few forms to the gentleman as well.

(POTTSY-WOTTSY *carries out the order imme-diately. Sweeps the remains of the cup and hurls them out the window, just like that, onto the pavement.)*

PROFESSOR: Are the fines very high?

POTTS: Fines? The breakers are awarded monthly prizes for social responsibility by the Ministry of the Production of Shards. If you're very successful, you can become an honorary member of the Master Breakers' Association! In response to my recommendation, of course. So can you, miss.

PROFESSOR: I feel rather unwell. *(Slumps into one of the three potti chairs.)*

(POTTER POTTS *motions to* POTTSY-WOTTSY, *who instantly pulls an enormous potti thermometer from his pocket and pushes it between* PROFESSOR*'s teeth.)*

POTTS: Sir, as you may have guessed, I am, above all, an entrepreneur. The operator of potti manufacturing processes, an inventor of new potti products. In other words, a potti know-all. Not the only one in Potteroonia, but the best of the best. Hardly surprising that my compatriots show respect for me which seems almost authentic.

ALICE: A master of self-praise!

POTTS: I want you to live in my house. However, you need to invent at least one potti product per

30

day. I'm offering you accommodation and food in return. *(Turning to* ALICE.*)* How about you, miss, what skills do you possess?

ALICE: None.

POTTS: Do you happen to play any instruments?

ALICE: Drums, but even that without any sense of rhythm.

POTTS: Can you sing?

ALICE: I prefer not to, because even my uncle can sing a lot better.

POTTS: Do you write poems?

ALICE: For the drawer. I haven't brought any with me because it's best for the drawer to stay in the desk, where it belongs.

POTTS: From now on, you will write poems for me. I declare you a promoter for the excellence of my potti products. You must compose a poem about potti earplugs by tomorrow.

ALICE: That's impossible. My poems are all about murmuring brooks, green glades and small clouds in the sky.

POTTS: There are no such things in our country. Here, everything's just potti, potti, potti. Regardless of how we've grown tired of this.

ALICE: But surely there must be things that can't be made of potti. Clothes, bed linen, forks, spoons?

POTTS: Everything. Even toilet paper.

PROFESSOR: *(Pulls the thermometer out of his mouth, feeling himself all over.)* I'm beginning to feel as though I were made of potti myself!

31

POTTS: *(Takes the thermometer from his hand.)* For-ty-two!

ALICE: Uncle! Are you all right?

(PROFESSOR stares blindly at the closest wall. ALICE waves a hand in front of his eyes. No reaction.)

POTTS: This gentleman is suffering from the initial stage of potti fever. It seems the vaccine didn't work.

ALICE: I know all diseases, but I haven't heard of this one.

POTTS: Potti fever is a mental derangement resulting from a sudden confrontation with potti logic.

ALICE: Is it dangerous?

POTTS: It may have some unpleasant consequences.

ALICE: What kind?

POTTS: The patient who hasn't fully recovered may turn into a Pottsy-Wottsy. My Pottsy-Wottsy used to be a man of average intelligence. Then he succumbed to the fever, and now the consequences are all too obvious. Aren't they, Pottsy-Wottsy?

POTTSY-WOTTSY: Yes, yes, they are. I'm the consequence of the result. Or the result of the consequence, I cannot tell. Maybe both. Haha! I'm very happy. It's nice to be a Pottsy-Wottsy. Carefree. Effortless. *(Raises his arms and slaps himself on the thighs.)*

ALICA: But I don't want my uncle to become a Pottsy-Wottsy! Give him some medicine! Take him to the doctor!

POTTS: There's just one kind of medicine: The patient needs to become a qualified potter. That will make all the symptoms disappear for good. The courses are not demanding and the lectures can begin right away. For both of you at the same time.

ALICE: I have no intention of becoming a qualified potter.

PROFESSOR: *(Suddenly comes to life and stands up.)* Neither have I. No offence, but I'm an economic advisor and I plan on remaining one.

ALICE: *(Applauding.)* Well done, Uncle!

POTTS: If you're not a qualified potter, you'd be as useful to me as a flea to a rabbit. Everybody's a qualified potter in Potteroonia, even Pottsy-Wottsy. Rest assured I'll teach you everything I know.

PROFESSOR: You're going to teach us?

POTTS: Who else? I'm the chief instructor!

PROFESSOR: No doubt you're also the Head of the Potteroonian Tourist Office.

POTTS: No, that's Pottsy-Wottsy.

PROFESSOR: That's hard to believe, considering the gentleman's mental capacities.

POTTS: That's reason enough. Since the last tourist here was sighted five years ago, the post is ideal for Pottsy-Wottsy, as he doesn't have to go to the office because of a total absence of work.

POTTSY-WOTTSY: Total absence!

PROFESSOR: What a pity. I was hoping he would tell me the name of the best restaurant in Pottington.

POTTS: The best restaurant in our city is called The Fish.

PROFESSOR: Where can we find it?

POTTS: On any corner. All the restaurants are called The Fish. They are all the best, all serving the famous Potteroonian dish: grilled fish.

ALICE: I don't like fish.

PROFESSOR: Neither do I. Where can we get something else?

POTS: Nowhere. One of the side effects of our economic miracle was the complete destruction of all animal and plant species. Including, thank God, lice and fleas. Therefore, everybody who does not wish to die of hunger eats fish. Unfortunately, I don't like fish very much myself, that's why I am, as you may have noticed, far less bulky than Pottsy-Wottsy. He doesn't like fish either, but as a result of potti fever, he thinks he's eating beef instead of fish. And since he likes beef, he just can't stop.

ALICE: Listen, sir! *(Reciting a poem.)*

> *Professor and I*
> *are not here for a lark,*
> *and even less so*
> *to eat sardines,*
> *so I'm telling you straight*

it's getting rather late
for Professor to flee,
including me.

POTTS: Brilliant!
POTTSY-WOTTSY: Brilliant!
ALICE: Uncle, one, two, three, off we go!
PROFESSOR: *(Stares at the hustle and bustle in the square, then turns around.)* Listen, Alice, even in the life of a twelve-year-old girl there comes a moment when she needs to act in an adult and responsible manner.
ALICE: The adult and responsible manner is to get away from here as soon as possible! The people here are completely nuts.
PROFESSOR: It's my obligation to save Potterooni- ans from ultimate destruction. And yours is to help me to the best of your ability.
ALICE: I left my best abilities at home.
PROFESSOR: When it's impossible to step back, it's necessary to step forward, if only into the unknown.
ALICE: *(Wiping her tears.)* What does that mean?
PROFESSOR: It means that I'm going to enrol in the training programme for potters, and you're going to write a poem about potti earplugs.
ALICE: I won't.
PROFESSOR: You will.
ALICE: I won't.
PROFESSOR: You will.

ALICE: *(Gives up.)* All right. When do we start?

POTTS: Right now.

PROFESSOR: On one condition, Mr Know-All Potts. You must introduce me to the members of the Potteroonian high society.

POTTS: Nothing easier. You have the Potteroonian high society standing right in front of you!

Scene Five

POTTS *motions to* POTTSY-WOTTSY *who pulls a brownish tablet out of his pocket and starts reading.*

POTTSY-WOTTSY: The person standing before you is one of the principal architects of the Potteroonian economic miracle. His posthumous monument will be extremely large. After being relocated underground, it will support the Earth's crust for at least one hundred years! The multiple Doctor of Science and Honorary Professor Potter Potts takes so much credit for the dynamics of our economy it's almost impossible to praise him too much. It is to his credit that almost everything is made of potti today. We can all remember the days when potti was just filthy clay from which cheap pots and other junk were produced. Today potti is the substance our civilisation rests on. The only problem we increasingly face is the consequence of our success: how to make our civilisation last a bit longer. Therefore, the multiple genius Professor Potts, with his sense of responsibility for the island's destiny, has announced his candidacy for the President of the State of Potteroonia. This is the only position that will enable him to carry out reforms that will shift the burden of seeking a long-term solution onto the shoulders of our descendants. *(He puts the tablet back into his pocket.)* As chief of his election campaign, let me cheer: Long live Mr Candidate! Long live Mr President!

POTTS: Thank you, Pottsy-Wottsy.

PROFESSOR: All the way to the top and mercilessly forward. Congratulations. Alice, go ahead, make up a poem dedicated to the gentleman running for the presidential post.

ALICE: I can't because it will be the worst poem ever.

PROFESSOR: With a bit of luck it may be an average one.

ALICE: You'll regret it. *(Starts reciting.)*

When our candidate decides to tackle the matter,
with potti at play, things change for the better,
in his care for the nation he's never slack,
so let's help him along the presidential track.

POTTS: Splendid! Being a connoisseur of classical poetry, I cannot be but genuinely thrilled. It's a pity, miss, you can't sing it.

ALICA: If you want to hear something even worse, I may just as well sing it.

(She starts to sing; very poorly. PROFESSOR is embarrassed.)

POTTS: *(Thrilled.)* Thank you, miss! Thank you for demonstrating that the proposal I'm about to make is truly justified. I need a campaign leader. Somebody who knows how to make my ideas appealing to voters, while diverting them from the desire to check whether they can be realised.

POTTSY-WOTTSY: But Mr Candidate, I am the leader of your election campaign!

(POTTS gives him a slap and turns to ALICE.)

POTTS: Anyway, I need someone who won't drive my voters towards my rivals' camp by his or her appearance, but instead will lure other voters towards ours. This can only be you.

ALICE: Me?!

POTTSY-WOTTSY: Mr Candidate –

(POTTS gives him two slaps, the first one from the left, the second from the right, then he turns to ALICE again.)

POTTS: Yes, you, miss, along with your harmonious singing that Potteroonians can only dream of. In our country, everything has long been out of tune; no one can sing any more, no one reads poems, the last book of poetry was published ten years ago. You have brought into the dusty atmosphere of this city a touch of youth, joy and harmony, which will charm our population, filling even the greatest sceptics with the hope that there's a bright future ahead of us.

ALICE: I don't know what to say.

POTTS: *(Rubbing his hands.)* It's a deal.

ALICE: Mr Pottsy-Wottsy, you're still the leader of the election campaign. And I'm still my uncle's assistant. We signed a contract, and contracts are to be respected, aren't they, Uncle?

PROFESSOR: Mr Presidential Candidate, the problem is that Alice doesn't want to change her job and is willing to implement only my ideas.

POTTS: It's your ideas I'm counting on if my campaign is to be successful. So I suggest you join my team as the Minister of Economy!

POTTSY-WOTTSY: Mr Candidate, didn't you promise this post to me?

POTTS: You're right, Pottsy-Wottsy. And what are your ideas for a successful election campaign?

POTTSY-WOTTSY: *(Puzzled.)* Ideas … Ah … Wait … My ideas are … Ah! … I see … Ideas!

POTTS: *(Gives him two nasty slaps.)* Thank you, Pottsy, for your exceptional mental effort. No doubt you need some rest now. I suggest you finally make the tea we've been waiting for ever since our arrival.

POTTSY-WOTTSY: That was exactly my idea! *(Rushes to the adjacent room.)*

PROFESSOR: In short, Know-All Potts, you're offering me –

POTTS: As long as I'm satisfied, of course. Which depends entirely on you. Due to the shortage of time, I'll instantly summon a meeting of the Committee for the Preparation of the Election Campaign.

PROFESSOR: But prior to this, I'd like to set a condition or two myself.

POTTS: *(Offended.)* I'm the one who sets conditions around here. If everybody does it, we won't get anywhere.

(As if he has just thought of something urgent, POTTS delivers a sharp slap to PROFESSOR, who quickly retaliates.)

PROFESSOR: Indeed, Mr Candidate, this is not the way to go. All the more so because you'll never become a President without my help. Unless you have your own ideas.

POTTS: I do have them, but they all get stolen by my rival, the current President Potterspot, who's already beaten me once and who's convinced he'll be re-elected. He doesn't know I've found a way to steal his ideas!

PROFESSOR: Then why do you need Alice and me?

POTTS: Because his ideas are useless. They may take us another step closer to the great collapse.

ALICE: Oh, dear!

POTTS: Still, this time I'm going to sweep Potterspot into the dustbin of history. I have a weapon he hasn't got.

PROFESSOR: A potti bomb?

POTTS: Something worse. The emotional factor.

PROFESSOR: Have emotions not been turned into support pillars yet?

POTTS: Let's be honest. Potteroonians don't live, one would say, a life worth living. In the morning, they go to the potterhouse, behind the conveyor belt moving along potti products, then to the supermarket to buy potti products, then into the smashhouse where they break potti products, then in front of the TV to listen about the lack of shards to make support pillars. The news is always followed by the address of the senile Potterspot persuading them that everything is all right. And it's the same every day! They miss something beautiful. Dreams. Freshness. Poems.

PROFESSOR: And you're going to provide them with that.

POTTS: Imagine a presidential candidate making an appearance before the Potteroonian people with a pretty, young, intelligent girl by his side. Potterspot would break down sooner than a potti car during a collision with a bulldozer!

ALICE: Oh dear!

PROFESSOR: But how could an intelligent young girl be connected to a presidential candidate?

POTTS: As a long lost daughter! Deposited on the Potteroonian coast by the high tide after a ship-wreck. Together with her uncle, the elder brother of a beautiful foreign lady who the presidential candidate met during a diplomatic visit to Paris twelve years ago.

ALICE: Uncle, may I remind you once more that we're headed for Trinidad and Tobago?

POTTS: Her mother died tragically, whereas the father neglected the daughter. I'm asking you: How can any Potteroonian woman resist such a story? And is there a Potteroonian man that wouldn't vote the way his wife ordered him to? I believe our move to the presidential palace is only a matter of time!

(Still seated, ALICE *and* PROFESSOR *look at each other, sipping the tea that* POTTSY-WOTTSY *has poured into their cups.)*

POTTS: Pottsy, what kind of tea have you made for us? Miss Alice and Professor have turned white as if on the verge of fainting. *(Delivers* POTTSY-WOTTSY *a slap.)*

PROFESSOR: *(Puts the cup back and gets on his feet.)* Mr Presidential Candidate, are you aware of who Miss Alice actually is?

POTTS: Your niece.

PROFESSOR: Not only that.

POTTS: Your secretary.

PROFESSOR: Not only that.

POTTS: Your assistant. We can agree on the price, I'm a generous man.

PROFESSOR: Are you aware that she fell down a rabbit hole as a child and became famous all over the globe? That the two books written about her are still being reprinted? At the age of twelve, she graduated from three universities. And in one of her MA theses she tried to prove, without success, of course, but extremely boldly, that two moments can exist not only in succession, but also simultaneously. Her friends are important and well-known personalities, such as Humpty-Dumpty, the White Queen, the Mad Hatter …

POTTS: As I said, name the price.

PROFESSOR: My niece is not for sale.

POTTS: Are you rejecting my offer?

PROFESSOR: What if I am?

POTTS: In that case, the rule requires that Pottsy puts a hand grenade between your legs and detonates it in such a way that the sharpest fragments will fly vertically upwards. Pottsy?

(POTTSY-WOTTSY *rushes into the adjacent room and returns with a grey machine reminiscent of a clock, ticking loudly. He carefully places it between* PROFESSOR*'s legs.)*

POTTS: Since I am, among other titles, a degree holder in human sciences, I'll act humanely. You've got five minutes to think about it. When Pottsy and I come back, I want to see two things. First, the two of you being enthusiastic about my offer, and second, your enthusiasm being sincere!

(Beckons to POTTSY-WOTTSY *to retreat with him to the adjacent room.)*

Scene Six

PROFESSOR: *(After a long pause.)* Five minutes is not really very long, compared to eternity.
ALICE: Leave philosophy alone, Uncle, it doesn't match the colour of your socks.
PROFESSOR: I wasn't expecting you to wait quietly and watch a time bomb ticking between my legs.
ALICE: Uncle, you said it yourself, I'm not for sale!
PROFESSOR: In a few minutes, we'll be processed into material for support pillars.
ALICE: So be it.

44

PROFESSOR: Alice, you can easily imagine acting the part of a long lost daughter on a school stage, can't you?

ALICE: No.

PROFESSOR: Would you really like us to vanish from the story before it even begins?

ALICE: I am just being stubborn. And I don't know where this stubbornness comes from. Help me, Uncle. Do something!

PROFESSOR: If a twelve-year-old girl decides to be stubborn, there's no remedy for it.

ALICE: What if I just give it up?

PROFESSOR: The thing is you can't, despite yourself.

ALICE: You're right, I can't. I'm sorry.

PROFESSOR: We could open the window and jump out on the street – we're both Jumpers, aren't we? Anyway, we should have thought of this earlier, it's too late now.

ALICE: Maybe not. Maybe I should jump to the window and open it, and then we'd both jump and fly off to the other side of the square. And from there onwards, like a pair of grasshoppers.

(ALICE *jumps to the window, but before she manages to open it, a horrible noise starts on the square: a mixture of ringing, sirens, screaming, running and general chaos, making it all sound as though the end of the world has arrived.)*

PROFESSOR: What's going on? *(Still not daring to move from his position so as not to activate the bomb by mistake.)*

ALICE: The people are bustling about, screaming, 'We're falling, falling, falling!'
PROFESSOR: Here we go.
ALICE: *(Quickly crawls under the table.)* Uncle! If you care for me at least a little bit, do not let the ground beneath our feet collapse!
PROFESSOR: What do you want me to do?
ALICE: We must fly away!
PROFESSOR: An excellent idea, but we have no wings.

(POTTER POTTS and POTTSY-WOTTSY come back from the adjacent room. Although they can hear the clamour coming from the square, they are perfectly calm.)

PROFESSOR: Hey, we're falling! Are you not afraid?
POTTS: Afraid of what? Of the stupid exercises the half-witted Potterspot has thought of?
ALICE: *(Crawls out from under the table.)* Exercises?

(POTTS beckons POTTSY-WOTTSY.)

POTTSY-WOTTSY: President Potterspot has issued a decree stipulating that every so often an alarm should be set off, such as used in case the Earth's crust begins to collapse.

PROFESSOR: But if this is repeated regularly, no-body will believe in the end that the alarm is real.

POTTS: Exactly.

ALICE: Where would we hide anyway?

POTTS: Nowhere.

PROFESSOR: I must say that your President should be shot for coming up with ideas a five-year-old child would be ashamed of. Mr Candidate, it's time we started thinking about the election campaign. Isn't it, Alice?

ALICE: If you say so, Uncle.

POTTS: Put the grenade away, Pottsy.

(POTTSY-WOTTSY *bends over, picks up the ticking object and flings it against the wall.* PROFESSOR *and* ALICE *stiffen, expecting an explosion. However, the "bomb" shatters like a china pot.*)

POTTSY-WOTTSY: I'll fill out the form – since I processed the bomb into shards!

POTTS: Sure, Pottsy. And now, clean up the mess. Also, bring a bottle of best potti spirits for us to propose a toast. And twenty glasses.

(POTTSY-WOTTSY *sweeps up the shards and carries them into the adjacent room, delighted.*)

PROFESSOR: Why twenty?

POTTS: I'd like to introduce you to some distinguished members of the Potteroonian elite, my closest friends.

Scene Seven

POTTS *claps his hands and suddenly, as if on command, people begin to enter the room one by one: a funny little man with a handlebar moustache pointing up, a stout lady with an abundance of muscles and a glare in her eyes, and another funny little man, very much resembling the first one, only with his moustache hanging down.*

POTTS: (*Introducing the first one.*) Mr Pottpott, the inventor of our vaccine against potti fever. The manager of our most luxurious hotel, Potteroonia, which offers the luxury of bed linen on top of the beds. President of the Committee for Connections with the United Media. Head of the Coordination Committee of the Association of Senior Smashers. The desk is yours, Mr Pottpott.

(The little man with his moustache curved steeply upward, having shaken hands with PROFESSOR after each sentence, also shakes hands with ALICE in the end. Then he lifts the desk and carries it to the adjacent room, from where a cracking sound can be heard.)

Mrs Potterola.

(The giant lady with a glare in her eyes steps forward without a word.)

The winner of the last Block Demolition Competition. An auxiliary speaker on the Potteroonian Radio. A surgeon specialized in the removal of pottifried gall bladders. A Support Pillar Quality Supervisor. Do take two chairs, Mrs Potterola.

(The lady picks up two potti chairs with her two little fingers, taking them to the adjacent room, smashing them against the wall with such force that a few particles end up rolling through the door. Then she returns with an unaltered facial expression and joins the queue.)

Mr Potteroonko.

(The little man with drooping moustache steps forward, swinging his head so violently that his moustache flaps.)

Minister for the Measurement of Material and Population Pressures on the Earth's Crust. Head of the Department for Granting Potti-Market Licences. An auxiliary expert for the mummification of corpses into support pillars. The last chair is yours, Mr Potteroonko.

(MR POTTEROONKO, dissatisfied by having received half less than his predecessors, grabs the chair and takes it to the adjacent room. There he smashes it against the wall. Then, judging from the noise, he starts to trample energetically on the shards. He returns and joins the queue.)

Let's continue.

(Beckons once again to the little man with the upright moustache.)

Mr Pottpott, Managing Director of the Fish Catering Company. The designer of the new model of pottiyota. The designer of the previous model of pottiyota. The inventor of the fabric made entirely from potti derivatives. A Senior Public Prosecutor.

(The little man takes a bow and joins the queue. The giant lady steps forward.)

Mrs Potterola, the State Collector of Unpaid Taxes. Senior Advisor to the Potteroonian National Bank. An expert in the beating of naughty children.

(The giant woman joins the queue. The little man with the drooping moustache steps forward.)

Mr Potteroonko, a judge of the Supreme Potti Court. An astrologist with a successful private practice.

A support pillar maintenance supplier. A lawyer with a private practice specializing in civil action concerning outbursts of anger resulting in serious personal injuries. An analyst of production orientations anticipating the moment of our end. The composer of the Goodbye Potteroonia March.

(POTTSY-WOTTSY *returns from the adjacent room, bringing a jug of potti spirits on a tray, along with twenty potti glasses.*)

And now, our everyday ritual!

(POTTSY-WOTTSY *pours the spirits into three potti glasses.* POTTPOTT, MRS POTTEROLA *and* POTTEROONKO *grab and down them in one go before flinging them against the closest wall. Then, they argue for some time about who threw their glass with the greatest effect, smashing it to the greatest number of pieces. [The actors should improvise here.]* POTTSY-WOTTSY *pours them three more glasses, so they grab them again, drinking up with even greater enthusiasm and flinging the empty glasses against the wall with righteous indignation. This time, their quarrel about who deserves higher acknowledgment is even greater, verging on shouting.* POTTSY-WOTTSY *pours spirits into three potti glasses for the third time. The three members of the Potteroonian high society knock them back at once, and this time, for a change, they fling them against the ceiling, where they break and fall down on the heads of the aroused potti destructors in pieces. "Me!" the little man with the upright moustache screams with excitement, beating his chest. "Me!" the little man with the hanging moustache screams, jumping with agitation. "Me!" Mrs Potterola croaks like a frog, raising her head proudly above the two little men.*

ALICE: Oh dear, eleven more glasses to go.

(At that moment, MRS POTTEROLA *knocks both little men down, jumping onto the first one, then the second one. Then she starts trampling on them with all of her weight, until they are almost flattened.)*

We're not used to such things in our country – somebody should intervene!
PROFESSOR: *(Shrugs his shoulders.)* I think that here we should accept everything as normal. Or at least familiar.
POTTS: Pottsy!

*(*POTTSY-WOTTSY *opens the window and tosses the three brawlers, one after another, onto the pavement.* POTTS *rubs his hands.)* Done. You've just met my closest allies. An agreeable bunch of people, don't you think?

Blackout.

ACT 2

Scene Eight

When the lights turn on, PROFESSOR *and* ALICE *are lying on the floor, sleeping.* ALICE *awakens and sits up. She shakes* PROFESSOR, *who yawns and sits up.)*

PROFESSOR: Why did you wake me up?

ALICE: Were you dreaming about something beautiful?

PROFESSOR: I was dreaming about how great it is not to have a choice.

ALICE: Indeed.

PROFESSOR: We don't have to choose whether to sleep on a soft bed or a hard one …

ALICE: No, because all beds have been processed into support pillars.

PROFESSOR: We don't have to choose from one hundred dishes on the menu –

ALICE: Except you don't like fish …

PROFESSOR: Of course I do.

ALICE: You're the one who threw up after our first meal, not I.

PROFESSOR: I have a sensitive stomach.

ALICE: Do you like the local customs?

PROFESSOR: What customs??

ALICE: Do you find it normal to buy a potti oven in the supermarket and then smash it on the pavement outside?

PROFESSOR: Completely normal.

ALICE: Uncle, this is not what one sees in the streets of Ljubljana!

PROFESSOR: That's for sure.

ALICE: In Ljubljana it's even less common for traffic police to direct two rows of cars against each other and then count the wrecks lying all over the place.

PROFESSOR: But this makes sense.

ALICE: Are you joking?

PROFESSOR: In consumer society, one has to consume. The more you consume, the more you need to produce; the more people have jobs, the more people have wages to survive. And more people can consume more.

ALICE: Who came up with this stupid idea?

PROFESSOR: The more Poteroonians run low on the last resource they still haven't exhausted, the greater the need to support the Earth's crust with pillars to prevent its collapse. In short, they have to speed up the destruction of what they're capable of producing and to speed up the production of what they need to destroy.

ALICE: Is there no solution?

PROFESSOR: Only in the short run. In the long run, the Potteroonian civilisation is doomed to go the way of all the others before it.

ALICE: And whose fault will that be?

PROFESSOR: *(Grimly.)* Honestly, Alice, we're up the creek without a paddle. Perhaps we've fallen into the future – a world the way it's going to be in one hundred, two hundred years.

ALICE: We must escape!

PROFESSOR: Where to? Foreign airplanes haven't landed on the island for ages and the few boats the locals have are only used for fishing. They are completely cut off from the rest of the world. If there still *is* such a thing as the rest of the world. Perhaps this is all that's left of it.

ALICE: *(Snuggling up to him.)* Oh, Uncle, why didn't we fall on an island populated by funny strange animals instead? Funny people are way too tiring.

PROFESSOR: As the Chinese sage put it before being beheaded: When in doubt, go with the flow.

Scene Nine

The room is transformed into a podium equipped with a microphone, with a roaring crowd gathered outside beneath the window. Two armed officers, one in red uniform, the other in blue, carry a trembling old man onto the podium. He is so weak that both officers need to grip him under each armpit to support him.

RED OFFICER: *(Shouts from the window.)* Ladies and gentlemen!

(The crowd, however, doesn't quieten. The officer in blue uniform rounds his hands in front of his mouth and shouts twice as loud as his red counterpart.)

BLUE OFFICER: Be quiet! *(Silence spreads across the square.)* Ladies and gentlemen! Let's have a round of applause for our dearest and most respectable President Potterspot!

(A lukewarm applause and some whistling can be heard from outside.)

RED OFFICER: Your speech, Mr President!

(Shakes the old man, who would have slid to the floor if not for the two officers holding him up.)

POTTERSPOT: I like listening to speeches. Has it started yet?
BLUE OFFICER: You're supposed to make it!
POTTERSPOT: I do, all the time, but it doesn't make any difference! Take me home – I'd like to watch pottivision. It's the Construction Day today!

RED OFFICER: That is what we're here for, Mr President! You're supposed to open it!

BLUE OFFICER: Don't you see all the cameras turned towards you? You don't want to make a fool of yourself, do you?

POTTERSPOT: A fool, me? The Great Construction Day is my idea! History will remember me for another one hundred thousand years! *(Turns soft.)* I've hardly had any ideas lately though. You know, I'm not all that young any more.

BLUE OFFICER: *(Digging in POTTERSPOT's left pocket.)* Where have you got it?

RED OFFICER: *(Digging in POTTERSPOT's right pocket.)* Where do you have your speech?

(They grab POTTERSPOT by the feet, lift him in the air with his head hanging down to the floor, shake him vigorously a few times, then some more, as if emptying the contents of a sack. They keep doing this until a folded piece of paper drops out of POTTERSPOT's jacket. They place him back on his feet. The officer in blue picks up the piece of paper, spreads it and pushes it into POTTERSPOT's hands.)

Read it!

POTTERSPOT: I can't see anything. *(BLUE OF-FICER puts a pair of pottiglasses on his nose.)*

Ah! The speech! And people say I can't remember things anymore.

RED OFFICER: Just go ahead, Mr President!

POTTERSPOT: *(Half-heartedly.)* Potteroonians! *(Then something like disbelief creeps into his tone.)* Potteroonians! At the beginning of the Great Construction Day … Potteroonians! At the beginning of … At the beginning of the Great Construction … *(Suddenly, he stops, staring into space as if lost in thought.)* I've read this speech somewhere before.

RED OFFICER: Of course. At the opening of the last Great Construction Day.

BLUE OFFICER: And all the previous ones.

RED OFFICER: You've been reading this same speech at the opening of the same event for five years. Nobody wants to write a new speech for you.

POTTERSPOT: Nonsense! Nobody in Potteroonia has quite as much imagination as myself! I won't be offended by the army whose commander-in-chief I happen to be. Would you like to become a pair of support pillars?

(The officers pull their arms from under his armpits for a second; POTTERSPOT reels, on the verge of collapsing when the officers grab him again.)

BLUE OFFICER: The speech!

RED OFFICER: Now!

POTTERSPOT: *(Reading.)* Potteroonians! At the beginning of the Great Construction Day, a third one this year and by no means the last one, I wish to reiterate the fundamental significance of this unique event. Can you remember the motto I invented for the first event of this sort?

BLUE OFFICER: For the sake of the nation, demolish the house of your neighbour!

POTTERSPOT: Exactly. For the sake of the neighbour, demolish the house of your nation! Let today's event proceed in the spirit of the legendary Potteroonian bigotry, enviousness, stubbornness and wickedness. The more things end up being broken, the … the …

RED OFFICER: The sweeter the dreams of all Potteroonians at night.

POTTERSPOT: The dreamier the sweets of all Potteroonians at night! *(Turns around.)* Now what?

BLUE OFFICER: Home, Mr President.

RED OFFICER: To watch pottivision.

(They lift him off the ground and carry him offstage. In the meantime, a radio broadcast can be heard; the voice of a reporter in the foreground, the roaring of clattercars in the background.)

REPORTER: There we go! Twenty-seven shiny, new, undamaged models of Pottiyota – a spectacle beyond compare in the history of pottisport. They keep

59

crashing into one another sideways, from the front, from the back; and now we can see a second wave of racing vehicles approaching, with one hundred vehicles from the third wave rolling towards them from the other direction; they'll meet in the middle at any second, oh, that'll make it sound like the end of the world, the crowd is growing hysterical, and here we are: They've crashed!

(The sound of a mass collision of clattercars. Suddenly, POTTER POTTS and his closest allies: POTTSY-WOTTSY, MRS POTTEROLA, MR POTTPOT and MR POTTEROONKO mount the podium. POTTER POTTS makes a beckoning sign and PROFESSOR and ALICE join them. The clattercar broadcast comes to a sudden end.)

POTTS: My dear Potteroonians, allies, friends, all of you whose eyes are turned towards the future!

(The crowd's blood is boiling outside: at least a thousand voices scream, "Booooooooooooooooooooooo!" A few pairs of potticlogs land onstage. "Game, game, game!" repeat the persistent voices from among the crowd.)

You're right! May the best man win! I've decided that on this very day, which vividly symbolises the futility of old views regarding the ground beneath our feet, I will put an end to the speculations as to whether I will run for President of the State of Potteroonia, so I announce to the entire world that my candidature is now official. *("Well done!" shout some voices in the crowd, "Boooooooooooo!" howl the others.)* With your help, I will endeavour to return this land to what it used to be before our short-sighted politicians, in love with their own profit, had taken it to the brink of destruction. *(A smattering of heavy applause is heard from outside.)* If there are still some among you who distrust me, I wish to send you a message: Judge people by their deeds, not their promises. In the past five years, we've heard so many promises we could support the Earth's crust with them forever. Therefore, dear compatriots, let me introduce to you a gentleman who's going to become our Minister of Economy following my election victory. This is the world-famous advisor, Dr. Jumper, who has an ocean of ingenious ideas. *(PROFESSOR steps forward and takes a bow, meeting general acknowledgement.)* Not only has Professor Jumper saved countries such as China, USA, Zimbabwe, Tajikistan and Burundi from inevitable doom, which is itself a good enough accomplishment for the largest monument in Potteroonia to be erected in his honour, but Professor Jumper has become a qualified potter in record time! What's more, he was elected a member of the Academy of Master Breakers! *("Well done!"*

roars the crowd outside.) And now, my dear Potteroonians, I'd like to introduce to you a young lady
that will become a role model for all generations.
Ladies and gentlemen, a qualified potter, a poet and
a chanson singer, a star of the Potteroonian future,
Miss Alice!

*(ALICE takes two steps forward, takes a bow and
starts to sing horrendously.)*

ALICE:
> *Potti alarm clock*
> *is not only the horn*
> *of a new day,*
> *it is also the lock*
> *of a world*
> *about to be born ...*

*("About to be born ..." the crowd contributing the
chorus.)*

> *Potti alarm clock*
> *never hesitates,*
> *it likes to run amok –*
> *when the dawn breaks,*
> *it always explodes,*
> *announcing the start*
> *of a new day ...*

("Of a new day ..." the crowd contributing the chorus. A roar of applause breaks out. POTTER POTTS *smiles with satisfaction while* ALICE *feels embarrassed.)*

POTTS: My dear Potteroonians, only a brilliant economist such as Professor Jumper could have invented a disposable alarm clock that wakes you up by exploding. Half a million items have been sold thus far. And only a brilliant chanson singer such as Miss Alice could have climbed to the top of the Potteroonian music charts with a song about this potti product. And only a farsighted politician such as your candidate for the presidential post could have secured absolute loyalty from such a pair of exceptional people. *(Another round of applause, no whistling, no grunting.)* And finally, my dear Potteroonians, a news item that will soften at least half of your pottifried hearts. When our country still exported and imported and I travelled a lot to faraway countries, the most beautiful thing in my life happened. I fell in love. Yes, I fell in love with the younger sister of our future Minister of Economy, Prof. Dr. Jumper, who is standing next to me. A girl called Alice was born. But then my contact with the outside world was interrupted and so Alice remained overseas, lost. Until a miracle happened and she decided to look for her father herself. And here she is. Along with her uncle, who accompanied her. Alice wants to be with her father, stand by his side in the hardest of moments and help him save this island from ruin. *(Turns around, grabs* ALICE *by the hand and pulls her forward. They both take a bow before the crowd. This is followed by a round of applause, full of admiration.)* Journalists for women's magazines may arrange their interviews with Pottsy-Wottsy; first come, first served. I'm leaving now, my dear Potteroonians, for we have plenty of responsible work to do. Long live the future!

("Long live the future!" roars the crowd.)

Scene Ten

The expert team meeting in Potts' house. POTTPOT, POTTEROONKO, POTTEROLA, ALICE *and* PROFESSOR *are sitting on potti chairs.* POTTER POTTS *paces in front of them, back and forth.* POTTSY-WOTTSY *stands by his side, waiting obligingly for instructions.*

POTTEROONKO: *(Stands up.)* Mr Candidate, considering the support you're enjoying, your victory seems practically secured.
POTTS: Practically maybe, what about theoretically?
POTTEROONKO: *(Sits down woefully.)* I wouldn't know.

POTTEROLA: If you don't, you'd better be quiet.

POTTS: We cannot afford a single wrong move.

POTTEROONKO: I agree.

POTTEROLA: Oh, now all of a sudden, you agree.

POTTS: Old Potterspot may give the impression of being dead, but this could be no more than a ploy.

POTTEROONKO: I haven't thought of this possibility.

POTTEROLA: Or any other.

POTTS: Pottsy, have you got the Professor's latest invention?

(POTTSY-WOTTSY nods enthusiastically and reaches into his pocket. POTTS turns to the block demolition winner.)

Mrs Potterola, would you mind if Pottsy-Wottsy tried this invention on you?

POTTEROLA: I'd be most honoured.

POTTS: Raise you head and close your eyes.

(After POTTEROLA does this, POTTSY-WOTTSY pulls an elongated potti object from his pocket and breaks it on POTTEROLA's head with a heavy blow.)

POTTEROLA: And why is that?

POTTS: Because you talk too much and say too little. Have you got any more of these, Pottsy?

POTTSY-WOTTSY: Enough for everyone! *(Instantly breaks a similar object on* POTTPOT*'s head.)*
POTTPOT: And why me?
POTTS: Because you talk too little and say too little.
POTTEROONKO: Speaking of myself, I'd say I say just enough …

*(*POTTSY-WOTTSY *hits him on the head with the elongated potti object.)*

POTTS: Isn't this great? *(Reaches into* POTTSY-WOTTSY*'s pocket, pulls out one of the potti objects and breaks it on* POTTSY-WOTTSY*'s head.)* Potti silencer! Professor actually invented it because we got tired of slapping, but it immediately became clear that he succeeded in combining comfort with convenience. At last, order will prevail in our business, social and intimate relations! Production hardly manages to keep up with the demand. Between you and me, even Potterspot has ordered three lorries of silencers. Obviously, he can't find a better way to silence the sceptics in his party.
POTTEROONKO: Which is yet another evidence of –
POTTS: *(Interrupting him.)* Now I want to hear how I can win the election. You'd better be quick and tell me the best way or I will change the entire election team.

POTTEROONKO: *(Stands up.)* We've got to in-crease the amount of support material. If we remove the inner walls in all our buildings, both national and private, it should do for another year at least.

POTTS: What about the paintings, lights, coat han-gers – do you think they'll hang on their own in mid-air? *(Motions for POTTSY-WOTTSY to break another potti silencer on* POTTEROONKO*'s head.* POTTS *looks at* POTTPOT.*)* Go on!

POTTPOT: *(Stands up.)* I've got a very good idea. The city should gradually move underground. This way, the Earth's crust will rest on factory chimneys and the walls of the highest buildings. Then we can restart building because the new buildings will no longer be a burden, but additional support.

POTTS: No way.

POTTPOT: Well, actually, the idea is not really worth …

(Before he sits back, POTTSY-WOTTSY *breaks a silencer on his head.)*

POTTS: Madam, the winner of the Block Demolition Competition.

POTTEROLA: *(Stands up, clears her throat.)* People aren't performing their duties. All unbroken objects need to be taxed.

(POTTSY-WOTTSY stands on his toes and breaks two potti silencers on her head. POTTEROLA takes her seat, perplexed.)

POTTS: Is this all an expert committee is able to come up with? If you dare qualify the rubbish I've just heard as ideas, I can ask Pottsy-Wottsy for advice instead.

POTTSY-WOTTSY: I've actually got an idea, Mr Candidate. I've thought of a system of gigantic balloons extending from one side of the island to the other, each balloon attached to the hook in the ground, all of them holding the Earth's crust up in the air.

POTTS: Have you got any more silencers?

(POTTSY-WOTTSY pulls a potti silencer from his pocket and breaks it on his head.)

POTTSY-WOTTSY: But I quite like the idea.

POTTS: It's crap, like all the other ones! I'm surrounded by nothing but Pottsy-Wottsies! How can I hope to win, with elections three days away? Which means that for the hundredth time I'll have to rely on the advice of my famous economic advisor.

(PROFESSOR slowly rises to his feet, walks across the room, walks around POTTEROONKO, POTTPOT and POTTEROLA. Then he starts to speak so quietly everyone has to lean forward.)

PROFESSOR: Pottsy's idea for producing balloons, though a stupid one, gave me a brilliant idea. When the ground collapses, the island will disappear and the cave beneath us will be flooded by the sea. Ergo: We can only be saved by wearing lifebelts.

POTTS: Mr Potteroonko, how do you like the idea?

POTTEROONKO: I have no special opinion, Mr Candidate.

POTTS: A minister without an opinion is not a minister. You've just lost your position. Sit down. And you, Madam?

POTTEROLA: Theoretically, it's not a bad idea, but there are two million Potteroonians. Who will manufacture such a number of lifebelts?

POTTPOT: And each of them would need at least two spare ones. It is well known that lifebelts tend to leak, they might even burst.

POTTS: Pottsy-Wottsy!

(First, POTTSY-WOTTSY *silences* POTTEROLA, *then* POTTPOT; *they both sit down.)*

All three of you are going to become Ministers of the Curdled Brain! Who will produce so many lifebelts? Me, who else? Not me personally, but my pottifactories. The less durable they are, the faster and more massively they'll have to be produced. Mr Professor, not only have you just earned me pottimillions, but, politically speaking, your idea seems so brilliant that Potterspot can count only on the vote of his pottifried aunt, and even that is questionable. We've won! *(His eyes linger on* ALICE.*)* Miss Alice, I think we deserve a song!

ALICE: *(Singing.)*

> *What harm can they do,*
> *can they do, can they do to us –*
> *we have plenty of lifebelts;*
> *and we can inflate them,*
> *we can deflate them,*
> *we can lie down on them –*
> *what harm can they do,*
> *can they do, can they do to us ...*

Blackout.

Scene Eleven

Some time has passed. The Steering Committee meeting again. POTTIELA, in high heels, comes mincing through the door. She walks straight to ALICE, proffering her hand.

POTTIELA: I so admire your voice!
ALICE: Oh, thank you!
POTTIELA: It reminds me of the cat I used to have before all the cats were turned into support pillars.

When I stepped on its tail, accidentally or deliberately, it would meow the way you sing. However, this should not divert you from making a career in this field. Considering that Potteroonians are completely tone-deaf, your success is more or less guaranteed. If we disregard the occasional moan resulting from digestive problems, you're the only singer on the island.

ALICE: *(Covering her face with her hands.)* How horrible!

(POTTIELA approaches POTTS, who has retreated into a corner, hands raised in front of his face. POTTIELA starts taking potti silencers from her handbag and breaking them, one by one, on POTTS' head.)

POTTIELA: Bastard! … Villain! … Traitor! … Good-for-nothing! … Son of a bitch! Potthead! *(Kicks him.)* You flea! … You piece of shit!

POTTS: I owe you … and others an explanation …

POTTIELA: You owe *me* one, you cockroach, and I'll explain to the others and also to you, in case you've forgotten, *what* you owe me!

POTTS: Pottsy, what are you waiting for?

(POTTSY-WOTTSY advances boldly towards the enraged young lady, but before reaching her, POTTIELA makes a step towards him and hits him on the head with her handbag several times.)

POTTIELA: Don't you dare come closer than a mile to me!

(POTTSY-WOTTSY *retreats into a corner.)*

POTTS: Pottiela, can't we discuss this in private?

POTTIELA: *(Turns towards the company.)* In return for the promise made by this liar to marry me and make me the First Lady of Potteroonia, I spent two weeks with that old cripple Potterspot to get details out of him about his election campaign for the Know-nothing Potts, so he could come up with a better one.

POTTS: Pottiela …

POTTIELA: That's how low I've sunk. Blinded by loyalty. And now I read in every newspaper a moving story about a long-lost daughter seeking him for years. And how her mother was the most beautiful woman in the world, and how he's never been so in love with anyone. And how no Potteroonian woman can compare to her! *(Turns to* POTTS *and slams her handbag on his head.)*

POTTS: Be realistic. You're just not suitable to be the First Lady of Potteroonia.

POTTIELA: Why not?

POTTS: *(Raising his voice a little.)* Because the Potteroonian First Lady should be beautiful, intelligent, sensible, mild, obedient and kind to everyone.

POTTIELA: Am I not all that?

POTTS: I haven't noticed. Neither has anyone else. Besides, the President's wife should be impeccable.

POTTIELA: What do you mean?

POTTS: My dear, you spent two weeks with Potter-spot –

POTTIELA: *(Slams him on the head with her handbag.)* My dear Potts, the president of the country should also be impeccable. At least in image. And your image will seem far less appealing to voters once I hold a press conference telling the world how you used and abused me. Unless, of course, you fulfil your part of the deal.

(Turns on her heels and leaves. Silence in the room for some time.)

POTTS: Is that all you have to say?

POTTEROLA: *(Plucks up the courage.)* Mr Future President, I could, with your permission, of course, break the lady's nose and a few bones. I could squeeze her kidneys, liver, lungs and other organs –

ALICE: *(Unable to control herself.)* Hey, what's that supposed to mean? What's the point of saving our civilisation if there's no civilised behaviour any more?

POTTS: Pottsy!

(POTTSY-WOTTSY takes a run, rushes through the room and slams into POTTEROLA's belly like

an enormous ball, knocking her to the ground; then he sits on her until she starts to suffocate. Finally, he crawls off her and gets to his feet.)

Well done, Pottsy!

ALICE: Uncle? What about that jump of ours that we've been contemplating for quite some time?

PROFESSOR: Too early for that. Everything will be all right.

POTTS: Nothing will be all right. If Potterspot wins, our presidential and ministerial positions will be nothing but cock-and-bull stories unfolding in the minds of ambitious fools.

POTTEROLA: *(Rises from the ground as if nothing happened.)* The question is what to do.

POTTS: I've thought of a solution! What does Pottie-la need? A man securing her reputation and social status. *(His eyes settle on the little man with the upright moustache.)*

POTTPOT: *(Briskly rising.)* I truly apologise. I have prostate problems for years and must go to the toilet a hundred times during the night. An awkward situation for my prospective wife. She wouldn't be able to get a good night's sleep.

POTTS: Don't worry, Mr Pottpot, it never entered my mind to put such a heavy burden on you. *(His eyes settle on the little man with the drooping moustache.)*

POTTEROONKO: I have … Well, I haven't anything like this that would … but I've got … I mean, I've been thinking, very seriously, about the possibility of getting engaged to a rather pretty traffic warden … it's not quite certain yet, but …

POTTS: Don't worry, Mr Potteroonko, not in my wildest dream have I thought of you as being a consolation prize for Pottiela; she would walk all over you on your wedding night! *(His eyes settle on POTTEROLA.)*

POTTEROLA: Well, I'm out of the question, for obvious reasons.

POTTS: The reasons may not be as obvious as you think. (*Glancing at her more masculine than feminine figure.*) But no, you're hardly an option. The only person who has a good enough position and reputation and, let's hope, all the rest intact, is our future Minister of Economy.

(Stops right in front of PROFESSOR, who would gladly have stepped backwards if he weren't standing right next to the wall.)

ALICE: Never!

PROFESSOR: Well, for the election campaign to succeed, I'm willing to make a few sacrifices –

ALICE: *(In disbelief)* Uncle!

PROFESSOR: However, when still in my cradle, my mother told me I should only surrender to a woman for whom I'd be the reward of a lifetime. As I haven't met any such woman, and most certainly won't, I haven't surrendered to any nor will I.

ALICE: Well done, Uncle!

POTTS: Are you aware, sir, that your stubbornness will condemn two million innocent Potteroonians to premature death? If Potterspot wins, his policies will lead to a cave-in in less than two months!

(Suddenly, POTTIELA returns. All of them stare at her in amazement.)

POTTIELA: I just realised I don't care for you, Potts. *(Walks up to him and hits him on the head with her handbag.)* Have your election campaign. Win and become President. I won't interfere. But in return, I want a real man!

(Grabs PROFESSOR by his hand and pulls him out the door before PROFESSOR can even think of resisting. ALICE cannot believe her eyes. Neither can the others.)

Blackout.

Scene Twelve

ALICE *and* POTTSY-WOTTSY.

POTTSY-WOTTSY: Why are you unhappy?

ALICE: Because time is moving too fast.

POTTSY-WOTTSY: Really?

ALICE: As soon as the day breaks, it already gets dark. As soon as the evening turns into night, clattercars are already roaring in the streets, with people rushing back and forth, screaming, "We're falling, we're falling!"

POTTSY-WOTTSY: A false alarm.

ALICE: Not any more. The ground is increasingly shaky.

POTTSY-WOTTSY: Personally, I like it. Why are you sad?

ALICE: I miss my uncle.

POTTSY-WOTTSY: Go and see him.

ALICE: I can't. Pottiela, who practically threw herself at him, is very jealous.

POTTSY-WOTTSY: Aren't you glad to have a room of your own in the palace of our new president, Potts?

ALICE: No, I'm not. I have to accompany him on all his visits, tours, patrols. I have to sing stupid out-of-tune songs. Besides, his popularity is declining sharply.

POTTSY-WOTTSY: Yes, his star is falling.

ALICE: And my uncle has fewer and fewer ideas about how to stabilise the Earth's crust.

POTTSY-WOTTSY: Go and see him.

ALICE: Do you think so?

POTTSY-WOTTSY: Go and see him.

ALICE: You're actually very kind-hearted, aren't you?

POTTSY-WOTTSY: I wouldn't know.

ALICE: Why not?

POTTSY-WOTTSY: Because I'm stupid.

Blackout.

Scene Thirteen

Lights. POTTIELA *and* PROFESSOR. ALICE *eavesdropping at the door.*

POTTIELA: This is the twenty-first silencer I've broken on your head!

PROFESSOR: *(Gloomily.)* And this is the twenty-first time you've interrupted my train of thought.

POTIELLA: I'll interrupt you on other things if you don't get moving. All you do is ruminate. What are you thinking about?

PROFESSOR: A plan to save our civilisation.

POTTIELA: Are you joking? You call letting others have what you deserve civilisation?

78

PROFESSOR: I'm not complaining.

POTTIELA: I wasn't thinking about you having me, you cockroach! That is certainly something to be proud of. You can be satisfied with this. What man has a woman standing behind him as solidly as I stand behind you? And what woman is stupid enough to stand behind a man who doesn't deserve to have a woman of my class standing behind him? *(Starts squeaking.)* How can you let me spend my best years as an ordinary wife of an ordinary Minister of Economy? Instead of doing something to make me the wife of the President of Potteroonia?

PROFESSOR: But you said you don't like him!

POTTIELA: Oh my God, you've turned into a real Pottsy-Wottsy since you became a minister! How can you be satisfied with that Know-nothing Potts strutting in the presidential palace, enjoying the privileges you and I should enjoy by all standards of common sense?

PROFESSOR: I have no intention of becoming President!

POTTIELA: I, on the other hand, have every intention of becoming the First Lady of Potteroonia. And you, Jumper, will help me. That's why I married you in the first place.

PROFESSOR: You married the wrong man.

POTTIELA: Don't worry. I have a plan – you just have to realise it.

PROFESSOR: *(Loses his temper, screams.)* I will, but not yours! *(ALICE peeps into the room and sees PROFESSOR jump to his feet and start breaking potti silencers on POTTIELA's head, two at a time.)* Although I'd prefer all of you to crash into the chasm you'd dug yourselves because of your wickedness, I'll do everything I can to save your lives, if not brains. I still don't have any idea how I will do this, but I'm not going to allow anyone to stand in my way. Not you, not Potts, not his toadies. Not the lack of ideas I've been suffering from ever since I started living with you!

(At that moment, POTTER POTTS, POTTSY-WOTTSY, BLUE OFFICER, RED OFFICER, POTTEROONKO, POTTPOT and POTTEROLA march in, all wearing lifebelts, inflated and fastened around their waists. ALICE joins the tail of the queue, making it seem she came together with them.)

Mr President! What an honour! The entire government! What can I offer you? We've run out of fish.
POTTIELA: Toadstools as well.

(POTTS snaps his fingers. POTTSY-WOTTSY grabs the nearest chair and places it in the middle of the room. Increasingly acting like a king, POTTS takes a seat. Following the example of the two

officers, his toadies stand straight behind him with
POTTSY *and* ALICE *alongside.)*

POTTS: I've been receiving letters that claim you're interfering with the natural flow of Potteroonian economy.

PROFESSOR: That's my duty. I'm the Minister of Economy.

POTTS: It was your duty to help me win the election. Now it's your duty to make your wife happy. And not to break silencers on her head.

PROFESSOR: We're doing our best to create as much support material as possible.

POTTS: Pottsy, who calls the shots in Potteroonia?

(POTTSY-WOTTSY pulls two silencers out of his pocket and heads towards PROFESSOR, carrying one in each hand. But POTTIELA gives him a sweet smile and beckons him to come to her. As if spellbound, he obeys, his face glowing with hope. POTTIELA whispers something in his ear. Then she whispers something in his other ear. POTTSY-WOTTSY's face beams with pleasure. He stands next to POTTIELA, pushes the two potti silencers back into his pocket and gives POTTS a defiant look.)

Damn feminine wiles! We're only wasting time. Ministers! Slaps! Five apiece!

*(POTTEROONKO, POTTPOT and POTTERO-
LA raise their hands and they all head towards
POTTIELA and POTTSY-WOTTSY. However, before actually doing anything, POTTSY-WOTTSY
breaks three silencers on POTTEROONKO's head
and slaps POTTPOT three times in a rush of energy,
while POTTIELA treads on MRS POTTEROLA's
foot with her high heel, tweaking her nose three
times to the left and three times to the right. Wretch-
ed, they return to their seats.)*

Where's my army? *(The two officers grab their
pottiguns, aiming them at PROFESSOR.)* You im-
beciles, don't kill my Minister of Economy, I need
him! Just kick him! Not the minister! Pottsy! Kick
his backside until he returns to me.

*(The officers head towards POTTSY-WOTTSY,
but fail to reach him because POTTIELA lures
them to her with a sweet smile. She whispers something in their ears. The officers nod their heads and
position themselves next to her, one on each side.
POTTS jumps to his feet.)*

If this is a coup attempt, I warn you I have weapons
at my disposal that none of you have the faintest
idea about!

POTTIELA: Come on, show them!

POTTS: Very well. Regardless of the promises my two officers received from a female person present here, I'm offering them a chance to rejoin me. They can do this by returning to their places and saluting the President as newly appointed commanders of his guard of honour. Promoted to the rank of colonels, ha ha!

(RED and BLUE OFFICERS look at each other, return to POTTS and give him a salute.) POTTS stands up and walks around POTTIELA with satisfaction.)

Evidently, the sound of fanfares seems to have more appeal than the sounds of an out-of-tune piano on which so many pianists have left their fingerprints.

POTIELA: Go hang yourself!

POTTS: As for you, Pottsy-Wottsy, subtle hints would be too much to understand without a brain transplant. So let me tell it to you straight: I've decided that you're to be the prototype of a new animal species. It's not good that Potteroonia has no beasts any more; the activities of the hunting association had to be abandoned altogether. We're going to develop you genetically into something between a monkey and a rat – a new type of hairy animal that will laugh stupidly all the time; we'll call it pottsy-wottsy. Congratulations, dear friend, you're going to become a pioneer of the new stage in the evolution of living creatures.

POTTSY-WOTTSY: *(Utterly confused.)* Thank you, Mr President!

POTTS: For God's sake, Pottsy! Remember whose fish you eat and go back to your place!

POTTSY-WOTTSY: *(Hesitating, exchanging looks with* POTTIELA.*)* I don't know, Mr President, I really do not know!

POTTS: Colonels, didn't we come here to have a much needed shooting drill?

(With a swift gesture, he pulls a pottirevolver from under his jacket and aims it at POTTSY-WOTTSY. The newly appointed colonels follow suit with their pottiguns. Nevertheless, POTTSY-WOTTSY is not frightened; he closes his eyes and covers his ears with his hands. POTTS puts away his revolver, the officers lower their pottiguns.)

Pottsy-Wottsy, after careful consideration I have decided to promote you to the position of Vice President. Which means that if I die before you, you will succeed me as President of Potteroonia. You have three minutes to decide.

POTTSY-WOTTSY: I already have! *(Returns swiftly to* POTTS*'side.)*

POTTIELA: You may have won the battle, but you'll lose the war!

POTTS: In short, Mr Minister of Economy, my government team and I would like to tell you a few ugly things in the nicest possible way. Ugly because they won't let me sleep, and in a nice way because we're all humanists, myself in terms of education and my colleagues in accordance with my decree.

(Looks at POTTPOT *and snaps his fingers. The little man with the upright moustache points an accusing finger at* PROFESSOR.*)*

POTTPOT: Too many products have served their purpose for too long.

POTTEROLA: There aren't enough *new* products.

POTTPOT: The minister can't keep up with people's demands.

POTTEROONKO: There's a serious lack of material for support pillars. How's the minister going to prevent us from plummeting down headfirst?

PROFESSOR: Well, I've invented lifebelts!

POTTS: The problem with the lifebelts – and that's by far the ugliest thing – is that they're too durable! Not only durable, but also indestructible! Are you aware that due to this serious mistake I have started dismissing employees?

POTTEROLA: To make matters worse …

POTTS: To make matters worse, we've realised that the new invention for harmonising mutual relations cannot be implemented successfully.

PROFESSOR: What invention?

POTTSPOT and POTTEROONKO: *(Raising their right hands.)* The awl!

POTTS: People have grown tired of slapping each other. Potti silencers have become a mere social ritual, like a cup of tea. That's why Mr Potteroonko invented a third form of expressing annoyance. If you wish to show someone they've crossed the border of your tolerance, you just pierce their life-belt with an awl. Mr Potteroonko, a demonstration, please. *(The two moustached little men each grab an awl and try to pierce each other's lifebelts. Without success.)* See what I mean?

PROFESSOR: But isn't durability the feature that makes it useful to have lifebelts in the first place?

POTTS: To have, perhaps. But not to produce. If they don't pay, we won't have them either.

POTTPOT and POTTEROONKO: And then what?

POTTS: Mr Minister, I suggest that you start modifying the main product of the Potteroonian economy. Lifebelts must deflate at the slightest stab of an awl. The entire stock of impenetrable ones should be destroyed instantly. *(Turns to* POTTIELA.*)* As for you, my dear, you know only too well that the President can sack a minister overnight. Mr Potteroonko won't think twice about replacing your husband. His being the Minister of Economy is the only reason people greet you on the street.

POTTPOT and POTTEROONKO: Not even once, let alone twice!

(POTTIELA sticks out her tongue at POTTS, who offers her a wicked smile. Then he turns to leave the room with his team.)

PROFESSOR: Mr President.

(Everyone listens. PROFESSOR steps into the middle of the room and assumes the posture of a Minister of Economy.)

POTTS: Yes?

PROFESSOR: Regarding the consolidation of the ground beneath our feet, I propose we no longer erect monuments in honour of distinguished people only, but also of lesser mortals.

POTTS: Ten monuments are already erected every day in my honour! If this doesn't do, one or two hundred should be put up!

PROFESSOR: *(In confidence.)* Let's forget for a second you're a president, Mr President. I propose a new industry for you: a production line of monuments. Everyone should be entitled to have their monument put up in a public place. They can order it in your factory for a decent price. Afterwards, they can display it before their friends and family members, and later move the monument underground at their own expense.

POTTS: Er … Um … Er … Um … *(Obviously fancies the idea. Then changes his mind.)* That's out of question. To see monuments of costermongers, shard sweepers and other people I can't stand, standing next to mine on every corner? Mr Minister, you can shove your idea where the sun doesn't shine. (*Turns around to really depart this time, as do all the others. Except for ALICE, who wishes to have a word with PROFESSOR.*)

POTTEROLA: (*Suddenly remembering.*) Mr President, we forgot something!

POTTS: (*Comes back.*) So we did. Mrs Potterola, whom I asked to be the Honorary Dean of the Faculty of Pottifrenology, has called my attention to another ugly thing.

POTTPOT and POTTEROONKO: Yes, yes!

POTTS: Tell me, Mr Inventor, if the next time we hear the ground rumble and it caves in, what exactly do you think will happen?

PROFESSOR: It's hard to tell.

POTTEROLA: The ruins will crush us including our lifebelts!

PROFESSOR: The thing is –

POTTS: You've sold me a product that I sell to unsuspecting customers under the name "lifebelt"! You make me play the public role of the saviour of the nation without actually being one.

POTTPOT in POTTEROONKO: Yes, yes!

PROFESSOR: The purpose of lifebelts is not to protect us from falling. Their purpose is to keep us afloat when the ground collapses and the sea floods the cave under the city!

POTTS: We'll fall so deep that none of us will stay alive!

PROFESSOR: Not all of us, that's true, but a few lucky individuals …

POTTS: We need balloons, Mr Minister!

POTTEROLA: Balloons!

POTTSPOT and POTTEROONKO: Balloons!

POTTS: You've got exactly twenty-four hours to come up with a model of a balloon that will lift us in the air as soon as we are about to fall! Or we are going to lift *you* in the air – on a rope!

(Turns on his heel and departs, head high. He is followed by all the others, heads even higher. Except for ALICE, who is hiding behind the curtain by the window.)

POTTIELA: *(Attacks* PROFESSOR *instantly.)* Can you see it now?

PROFESSOR: What?

POTTIELA: You have no choice but to get rid of that insect! Try to think normally for once. The two of us urgently need an ally in his camp.

PROFESSOR: But not Pottsy-Wottsy.

POTTIELA: Leave that to me. *(Heads for the exit.)* You get down to making balloons. Two will do. For you and me. The others may just as well tumble down to where they belong.

PROFESSOR: The only solution is to frighten Potteroonians to death.

POTTIELA: *(Turns around and comes back.)* Why?

PROFESSOR: Because they don't really believe the ground beneath their feet can collapse at any moment.

POTTIELA: So?

PROFESSOR: If they are made aware of this, they might change their habits. And then re-education could begin to preserve at least half the island.

POTTIELA: And how do you intend to frighten them?

PROFESSOR: I'll trigger a restricted cave-in of the Earth's crust for warning purposes.

POTTIELA: An excellent idea. I'll compile a list of Potts' factories, workshops, processing plants, warehouses, shops and banks.

PROFESSOR: That makes it more than half the city; that would be the end of the world!

POTTIELA: If you don't want to, I can do it with Pottsy.

PROFESSOR: Do as you wish.

(POTTIELA *departs, slamming the door behind her.* ALICE *steps from behind the curtain.* PROFESSOR *winces and stares at her.)*

ALICE: Uncle. How are you?

PROFESSOR: Great. I'm only afraid that things will get even better. What about you?

ALICE: I can hardly wait for things to get worse, so I don't have to put up with them anymore.

PROFESSOR: What do you suggest?

ALICE: You should produce three big balloons that will lift us in the air at the moment of the great tumble and take the three of us across the sea.

PROFESSOR: Three of us?

ALICE: Yes, the President, you and me.

PROFESSOR: Why the President?

ALICE: We won't manage to escape without him. I suggest that we take him with us and get rid of him once we land somewhere.

PROFESSOR: Not a bad idea.

ALICE: So?

PROFESSOR: First, I have to think if there's perhaps another option, an even better one.

ALICE: Yes, think about it. Take your time. There's no hurry. Still, if we happen to crash into the cave while you're thinking, I hope I fall on you. Because if you fall on me, there won't be much of me left despite the fact that you eat nothing but fish. What's your usual meal? A shark a day? Half a whale?

ALICE *turns around and leaves.*

Scene Fourteen

A meeting in the Government Palace. ALICE *is also present.*

POTTS: I've called this meeting for two reasons. Firstly, I've got the impression that something is going on behind my back. And secondly, because I have no idea *what* is going on. Well, are you just going to stand there and stare at me?

*(*POTTPOT *and* POTTEROONKO *pull out his chair and* POTTS *sits down. Takes a look at those present.)*

What are you doing here?
POTTEROLA: You've called a meeting.
POTTS: I know nothing about that. Why?
BLUE OFFICER: Because something is going on behind your back.
RED OFFICER: And you don't know what.
POTTS: Surely I'm not growing senile at my age? Is this a common fate of all presidents? I know what it is! They're putting something in my food. There's a traitor among us. Maybe even one of you. *(Looks towards the two officers.)* I promoted you prematurely. From now on, you're ordinary captains again. *(As though at someone's order, the officers aim their pottiguns at* POTTS.*)* I meant to say generals. *(The officers lower their pottiguns and*

salute POTTS first, *then each other.)* It's good to have the army on your side, isn't it, Pottsy-Wottsy? *(However,* POTTSY-WOTTSY *is not present.)* Where's Pottsy-Wottsy to help me with my treatment? *(*POTTPOT *and* POTTEROONKO *approach and each break a silencer on his head.)* Thank you, Mr Pottpotteroonko. From now on, you will get the first taste of everything that's put in front of me. Your President needs protection.

POTTSPOT and POTTEROONKO: Me or him?

POTTS: The first and the second taste then. In addition, there's something else I propose. Let's call a referendum on renaming of the republic. Potteroonia must become a monarchy. When we go into exile, which could be tomorrow, most countries will be more inclined to accept a king than a president. Kings are few. As for presidents, even societies for the protection of animals have them.

(Everyone raises their hands, including ALICE, *who discovered long ago that while waiting for the opportunity to escape, it is wisest to pretend that the thought of escape is the last thing on one's mind.)*

Ah, the bliss of democracy! What's more, I just remembered why I called this meeting. Mrs Potterola, what do you think is going on behind my back?

POTTEROLA: I've no idea, Mr President.

POTTS: Why then did I appoint you as the Head of the Secret Service?

POTTEROLA: I know nothing about that.

POTTS: Are you going soft in the head? Or did I forget to appoint you? One way or the other, it's your fault. Had I forgotten about it, you should have reminded me. Am I the only one who knows that our Minister of Economy has been crawling beneath our feet, checking the support pillars? And discovering that here, under my palace, there are ten times more of them than elsewhere? You morons! Don't you see we're facing a crisis?

POTTPOT and POTTEROONKO: We do, but what can we do?

POTTS: You're asking me? I'm tempted to have you shot. *(The officers instantly aim their pottiguns at the three government ministers.)* But not just yet.

POTTPOT, POTTEROONKO, POTTEROLA: Thank you, Mr President.

POTTS: *(Turns to ALICE.)* Alice, you're the only one who can help us. Try to persuade your stubborn uncle – *(PROFESSOR marches in from the door.)* This man looks terribly familiar to me. Is it Pottsy-Wottsy?

ALICE: No, it's my Uncle Jumper.

POTTS: *(Takes a close look at PROFESSOR.)* It's hard to tell. One meets so many people who look incredibly alike that they don't even know for themselves who they are! But all right: Because I received my education in the humanities, I'm willing to believe it's really my Minister of Economy. In fact, I'm glad because I can tell him directly: The balloon, Minister! The evacuation balloon!

PROFESSOR: I'd like to speak to you in private.

(POTTS *and* PROFESSOR *move away from the others.*)

POTTS: Tell me.

PROFESSOR: *(Whispering.)* I'm making three balloons for the escape of three important people. At the same time, I'm preparing a controlled cave-in of the Earth's crust in one of the outer suburbs – for warning and re-educational purposes.

POTTS: Warning purposes? *(Thinks about it.)* I agree, I totally agree!

PROFESSOR: On one condition. Alice should return to me and you should remove Pottiela – either to your palace or to prison.

POTTS: Done! Take your niece with you. She hasn't been of much help recently. Worse than that, I've been receiving anonymous letters complaining that she can't sing! Speaking of Pottiela, I refuse to have her under my roof, God forbid. Still, this shouldn't be your problem. I promise she won't be there to-morrow and that's it.

PROFESSOR: Thank you, Mr President.

POTTS: *(Rubs his hands.)* That's settled then. In two days, you will deliver to me a balloon capable of carrying two tons of goods across the ocean. Meanwhile, I'll compile a list of areas suitable for the cave-in. Excellent! Goodbye, Mr Minister.

Goodbye, my long lost daughter. You're lucky I'm tone-deaf!

(ALICE follows PROFESSOR out of the room, but hides by the door, eavesdropping on the meeting.)

Did you hear what the Minister of Economy told me?

POTTPOT, POTTEROONKO, POTTEROLA: To the last word.

POTTS: His plan will increase substantially the feeling of financial security of the government and make our rivals suffer greater damage than a magnitude-10 earthquake on the Richter scale!

POTTPOT, POTTEROONKO, POTTEROLA, OFFICERS: Well done!

POTTS: The mountain will labour and give birth to one hundred thousand church mice! And our socially conscious state will help them with concessional loans to rebuild their ruined housing!

POTTPOT and POTTEROONKO: That's brilliant!

POTTEROLA: I suggest a one-hundred-per-cent interest rate for the loans.

POTTS: I'm not going to lend money for free. Three hundred per cent is the lowest interest rate for the victims of natural disasters in Potteroonia.

POTTEROLA: I was thinking about one hundred per cent per month.

POTTS: Even the state, which is entitled to greed, should not be as greedy as that. I'll approve three hundred per cent.

POTTEROLA: Thank you, Mr President.

POTTS: All that remains now is to make a list of candidates for the loan guarantee. Or rather a list of candidates whose possessions will fall into the cave during the controlled disaster set up by our clever Minister of Economy. *(Rubs his hands.)* We will include, as you'll no doubt agree, the potti product manufacturers competing with my production. And all the production lines owned by senile Potterspot!

POTTPOT and POTTEROONKO: *(Jumping up.)* That's brilliant!

POTTS: Mr Pottpotteroonko, Mrs Potterola, you'll compile the lists according to my instructions. In addition, you'll inspect the support pillars under the residence of the Minister of Economy, who will also need a loan, won't he? Ha-ha! You two Generals will devise a plan on how the chosen support pillars can be destroyed.

RED OFFICER: By the mines, Mr President.

BLUE OFFICER: Which can be triggered from here. With a detonator.

POTTS: *(Watching them for a while.)* Is there a military rank superior to that of a general?

RED and BLUE OFFICER: Chief of the General Staff.

POTTS: You are hereby appointed to be the Chief and the General Staff. Decide between the two of you who will be what.

Scene Fifteen

A room without furniture. POTTEROLA *drags former President* POTTERSPOT *through the door, holding him under the armpit so he wouldn't collapse. They are followed by* POTTPOT *and* POTTEROONKO *and both generals. They are all followed secretly by* ALICE. POTTEROLA *makes* POTTERSPOT *sit on the floor.*

POTTERSPOT: It's nice they're cheering and greeting me so wholeheartedly. I've always been a popular president.
POTTEROLA: Not any more, neither popular nor a President.
POTTERSPOT: What am I then?
POTTEROLA: A pest to everyone, including yourself.
POTTERSPOT: I won't let myself be scolded by the nation whose history I've made for so many years. *(Sees both generals.)* Who are they?
POTTEROLA: The history you've made has brought us so far that the army is forced to seize power.
POTTERSPOT: *(Yawns.)* Can I go to sleep?

98

POTTEROLA: No, you can't, because the army needs political legitimacy. And because there's no one else, it has to make do with you.

POTTERSPOT: And what are you, sir? A General or the Chief of General Staff?

POTTEROLA: First of all, I'm not a sir, but a madam. Secondly, I'm not a soldier, but the future Prime Minister. Thirdly, think hard because we must explain to you what this is all about!

(RED *and* BLUE OFFICERS *aim their pottiguns at* POTTERSPOT.)

POTTERSPOT: I've seen this before. A ground-to-air missile, isn't it? Or rather a heavy mortar. No, it's a pair of nuclear torpedoes for sinking submarines!

POTTEROLA: We need your signature.

POTTERSPOT: Help me on my feet.

(POTTEROLA *motions the generals to come closer and lift* POTTERSPOT *to his feet.*)

Help me to the window.

(RED *and* BLUE OFFICERS *look at* POTTERO-LA, *who nods her head. They follow the command and back off.* POTTERSPOT *leans against the windowsill.*)

Come on, shoot me straight in the heart.

(RED and BLUE OFFICERS *look at* POTTERO-LA, *who buries her face in her hands and weeps.)*

An army that wants to seize power should not be afraid to shoot! Come on, you idiots. History cannot wait for a silly woman to cry her heart out because she's unable to realise a plan of her own making. Shoot me first, and then her!

POTTEROLA: *(Turns around swiftly.)* No! You're right, Mr Potterspot, I made a terrible mistake! And now I'm afraid, not knowing where to go for protection myself.

POTTERSPOT: With me, who else.

POTTEROLA: Thank you, Mr Potterspot, thank you.

POTTERSPOT: *(Raises his index finger.)* I have a better plan than all Pottses and Ministers of Economy together! I've been implementing it secretly for the past ten years.

EVERYONE: Ooooooooh!

POTTERSPOT: These lifebelts that helped Potts steal my power are nonsense. When it starts to thunder and rock, the wreckage will bury everyone, including their lifebelts. Take off my jacket.

POTTEROLA: Your jacket, Mr Potterspot?

POTTERSPOT: My jacket. To show you my brilliant invention.

(RED and BLUE OFFICERS *take off his jacket. It turns out that* POTTERSPOT *has a parachute-like object attached to his back.)*

POTTEROLA: An interesting waistcoat, Mr Potter-spot.

POTTERSPOT: It's a parachute, not a balloon! Not a lifebelt, but a parachute! With it, you can safely fall into the depths and land without breaking a single bone! We'll expose Potts' wily intentions and life-belts. We'll demand new elections and win! Who's with me?

EVERYONE: Everyone!

POTTERSPOT: Open the window.

(He makes three steps towards the middle of the room without collapsing. BLUE OFFICER opens the window. Everyone else takes a deep breath. POTTERSPOT retreats all the way to the door, still ajar with ALICE hiding behind it.)

Let's say the ground starts to tremble. The collapse is imminent. What will you do? You will jump high in the air, pull this handle, and the parachute will open and you will land among the ruins of the col-lapsed city without a scratch.

EVERYONE: Well done!

(POTTERSPOT is about to rush towards the win-dow, but suddenly goes weak at the knees.)

POTTERSPOT: I need help. *(Nobody moves.)* What are you waiting for? Throw me out of the window!

(They all look at each other and shake their heads.)
I want to prove how reliable my invention is. Lift
me up and throw me out! That's an order!
RED OFFICER: Mr Potterspot, we're on the sixth
floor.
POTTERSPOT: From where else can I do a parachute jump? From the basement?

*(BLUE and RED OFFICERS lift POTTERSPOT,
then run with him towards the window and fling
him outside. A strained silence follows. In this silence, something heavy drops on the pavement
and remains lying there. Silence for a while. Then
POTTEROLA, POTTEROONKO, POTTPOT, plus
BLUE and RED OFFICERS take flight. ALICE
rushes to the window and looks outside.)*

ALICE: Oh, dear! Uuuuncleeeeee! *(Rushes off.)*

Scene Sixteen

*A street corner. ALICE rushes round the corner and
stops, hides behind the corner, where she observes
POTTIELA beating POTTSY-WOTTSY on the head
with her handbag.*

POTTIELA: What have you done with the tablets
you should have given President Potts? The little
white pills that cause premature senility?

POTTSY-WOTTSY: The tablets or the pills?

POTTIELA: You idiot! With Potterspot, they kicked in immediately. But why is Potts still in his right mind? Why does he only lose his memory from time to time?

POTTSY-WOTTSY: I don' know, I really do not know.

POTTIELA: Did you eat them yourself?

POTTSY-WOTTSY: (*Reaches into his pocket and pulls out a yellow pill box.*) I've got some left.

POTTIELA: (*Takes the box from his hand.*) With you, being senile at birth, they should produce the opposite effect!

POTTSY-WOTTSY: That's why I ate them! To be competent for the presidential post when the time comes.

POTTIELA: (*Kicks him.*) What am I supposed to do with you? The time I've been waiting for half of my life is drawing near, and you're playing the fool!

POTTSY-WOTTSY: I'll stop!

POTTIELA: Will it help if I pretend I'm not dealing with an idiot, but a genius?

POTTSY-WOTTSY: Sure.

POTTIELA: Have you any idea what politics is? Have you any idea what power is? I devised my first plot at the age of fifteen when I decided I wanted to go far in life using my looks, not my brain. Now, at the age of forty, I realise I shouldn't totally neglect my brain either. To my great surprise, it seems more lasting than beauty.

POTTSY-WOTTSY: I see, I see.

POTTIELA: *(Gives him a slap.)* What can you see? You, who's never possessed either brain or beauty! Pottsy, if you leave me high and dry, I promise to drag you single-handedly into the cave under the city and pottifry you into a pillar under my own house!

POTTSY-WOTTSY: *(Raises two fingers.)* I promise I won't.

POTTIELA: Go and check on how many balloons the Professor has made. And find out where Potter Potts is testing his. Don't forget.

(She reaches into her handbag and gives him an awl. POTTSY-WOTTSY *grins and runs off along the road.)*

Scene Seventeen

A room in PROFESSOR's *house.* ALICE *rushes in and discovers that* POTTPOT, POTTEROONKO, POTTEROLA *and both* OFFICERS *are already there.*

POTTEROLA: I have to warn you, Mr Minister, that Potter Potts is devising a terrible plot.

POTTPOT: I last saw him testing a large balloon.

POTTEROONKO: I'm convinced he will escape across the sea at the crucial moment.

PROFESSOR: He won't be missed. General Staff, your report.

BLUE and RED OFFICERS: *(Saluting)*: The dynamites are in place. The detonators activated. The connection established. The triggers are here.

(They take five unusual devices out of a large bag, arranging them on the floor, one after the other.)

PROFESSOR: Excellent. Which of these should I press?

BLUE OFFICER: All of them.

RED OFFICER: For all the pillars to collapse at the same time.

PROFESSOR: The Steering Committee, please report on the location and the scope of the planned cave-in.

POTTPOT: The area south-east from the city centre.

POTTEROONKO: One hundred support pillars ready to be blasted.

POTTPOT: The scope of the cave-in: twenty square metres.

PROFESSOR: Have the inhabitants been evacuated?

POTTEROONKO: Under the pretext that, due to the weakness of the support pillars, certain measurements and reinforcements are required.

PROFESSOR: Excellent. What about pottivision, pottiradio and other mass media? Have they been activated for my post-sabotage lecture?

POTTPOT and POTTEROONKO: Yes, Mr Minister.

PROFESSOR: *(Rubs his hands.)* Now we just need the President to trigger the blast.

(POTTPOT, POTTEROONKO and POTTEROLA look at one another.)

POTTEROLA: As I said, Mr Minister, Potter Potts is devising a terrible plot. He is no longer to be trusted.

PROFESSOR: It's the President who needs to take the responsibility. I don't have the necessary powers, and neither do you. I suggest you find the President and bring him here.

POTTPOT, POTTEROONKO, POTTEROLA: Yes, well, if there's no other way …

(They leave, grunting, followed by BLUE and RED OFFICERS. ALICE steps out from the door corner.)

PROFESSOR: *(Genuinely happy to see her.)* Alice!

ALICE: We don't have much time. Where are the balloons?

PROFESSOR: What balloons?

ALICE: *(Stamping her feet impatiently.)* Grrrrr!

PROFESSOR: I made only one, actually. For President Potts, otherwise he wouldn't have approved the cave-in. The balloon is useless. It won't carry him across the sea. Still, if it does, the reform will be more efficient without him.

ALICE: Uncle! A ship that's sinking is not suitable for a shipbuilding reform!

PROFESSOR: *(Stubbornly.)* If I save this island, I can save the world. If I can't, my responsibility requires me, like a good captain of a sinking ship, to go down with it.

ALICE: What about me?

PROFESSOR: *(Daydreaming.)* In a year, trees will start to sprout on the island. We'll start closing down pottifactories. We'll plough the soil, sow wheat, plant lettuce, potatoes …

ALICE: *(Screaming angrily.)* All right then! The sooner, the better! I can hardly wait to fill up on chips! *(Pulls the nearest trigger. A faraway explosion is heard; a part of the city has collapsed, sinking into the chasm.)*

PROFESSOR: Oh, Alice!

(POTTPOT, POTTEROONKO, POTTEROLA and RED and BLUE OFFICERS drag POTTS into the room. Each officer is holding one of his legs, POTTPOT and POTTEROONKO each have one of his arms, whereas POTTEROLA is holding his head.)

POTTS: You started without me, you bastards! Put me down!

(With childish joy, he presses the detonator he un-expectedly takes out of his pocket. This time, the explosion resonates much closer; one can hear buildings being demolished, and then the gurgling of water.)

PROFESSOR: Oh my God! What's going on?
POTTS: *(Going berserk.)* Your brilliant idea to save the island is being realised! *(Takes another detonator out of the other pocket.)* All the factories and houses of my rivals will end up in the cave beneath us!
POTTEROLA: *(Running amok.)* No one can defeat me! *(A detonator ends up in her hand.)* This is for all the humiliations I had to put up with!

(Pushes a button. The sound of three explosions resonates in the city. ALICE gazes out of the window, staring, in terror, at the buildings collapsing on the other side of the street. The thunderous sound of the invading sea can be heard.)

POTTIELA: *(Rushes in from the door. She has a detonator in her hand as well.)* Look at this, senile Potter Potts! Say goodbye to your factories, shops, banks, treasuries. *And* your palace!

(Triggers the detonator. ALICE sees the back part of the city panorama disappear, the blueness of the sky shining in the background. PROFESSOR

throws her a lifebelt. ALICE *puts it on. She sees that* PROFESSOR *has already put on his. Not a second too soon because the ground starts to rock, the walls crackle, the house starts to collapse, followed by a seemingly endless fall into the depths, accompanied by the frightened screaming of* POTTS, POTTIE-LA, POTTEROLA, POTTPOT, RED *and* BLUE OFFICERS *and countless Potteroonians of lesser importance. When the crackling, rustling and splashing come to an end,* ALICE *and* PROFESSOR *realise they are rocking on the surface of a boundless sea. The island has sunk and Potteroonia has experienced the fate of Atlantis.)*

ALICE: I didn't know you saved two lifebelts.

PROFESSOR: Just in case. Two real ones. These won't be punctured by any awl.

(But evidently they are not the only lifebelts around, because at that moment POTTSY-WOTTSY *swims past wearing one of his own, talking to himself enthusiastically.)*

POTTSY-WOTTSY: Not a soul in sight! Not a soul in sight! Just Pottsy-Wottsy, President at last, after all the years of waiting. The President of State! *(Waves to* ALICE *and* PROFESSOR *in a dignified manner.)* Greetings, ladies and gentlemen of Potteroonia! Your president Pottsy-Wottsy is inviting you to a symposium on planning the reconstruction of the country. If you have any ideas, just send them to me. You don't? Okay, we'll just live without ideas. Which is not a bad idea at all! What joy!

(Reaches into the pocket of his soaked jacket, pulls out an awl and pierces his lifeboat. Air starts to escape from it, producing a whistling sound. POTTSY-WOTTSY *disappears underwater, wearing a broad smile. Only* ALICE *and* PROFESSOR *remain on the sea surface.)*

ALICE: Now what?
PROFESSOR: *(Looks around.)* We'll have to trust the wind.

Artistic Directors and, Above All, Teachers: Stay Away!

Peter Potteroonkowich

When the author of this play for teenagers (and – as he puts it – adults young at heart) asked me to write an afterword to this book, I said to myself: Why not? There is never a lack of people contending for my professional opinion, normally without offering any payment (this time was no exception). Nevertheless, in this particular case I was attracted by two things: the fact that the play depicts the inglorious end of my homeland, Potteroonia, and the fact that I know the author. Not personally, of course, but I do know his novels and plays, which, to tell you the truth, I am not particularly fond of (I won't bother enumerating the reasons). Still, they do have a certain literary value, even though in a world such as we have created, literature plays only a side role, if any at all. And quite rightly so; life is too short to devote even the tiniest portion of it to unprofitable pursuits.

To return to *Alice*: I saw this ridiculous play in a slightly different form many years ago on stage, perhaps in the town of Jesenice, perhaps even in Potteroonia, perhaps on Broadway (anything is possible), the difference being that Alice's name was Mona. A little earlier (or later), I heard an abridged version on the radio, certainly in Slovenia, but maybe also in Iceland, maybe even (who knows) on the BBC. And then, out of the blue, a novel entitled *Alice in Crazyland* appeared on the market! Some say it is very entertaining, witty and God knows what else (it was even nominated for some prize, but there are so many these days that none of them has any significance).

Let me be honest: the people who praise this author are making too big a deal out of it. The reason is obvious, so there is no point in justifying my opinion. Some good gags here and there – that is all he is able to produce. I agreed to write the afterword for one reason alone: I was warned by a few well-meaning acquaintances that the play addresses the downfall of the Potteroonian civilisation. Of course, the author has little knowledge of this tragic event, considering he has never been there. Relying on something writers like to refer to as imagination is a poor replacement for hands-on experience.

And what is he really trying to tell us about the closing stage of the Potteroonian economic miracle? That we ourselves had dug the hole we fell in? That we were stupid not to have realised such danger existed? It is not hard to be wise after the event. If the author knew where we were heading, he should have warned us. I would certainly have listened to what he had to say, even though the majority of Potteroonians might have not. Or is it that his facetious play might be a warning targeted at some other world, the one I had moved to before Potteroonia collapsed into the sea? Is the author trying to say we are well on the way to a similar ending? That the last human to vanish from this planet will be an imbecile very much like Pottsy-Wottsy?

I will come straight to the point: When I left Potteroonia and arrived to these liberal, humane parts, with an abundance of all kinds of knowledge and economic wisdom, I soon got the impression that not only had I moved here, but that the Potteroonian mentality had arrived with me (if not before me). It is not uncommon for me to feel that executive positions in most countries have been occupied by runaway Potteroonians who failed to detach their minds from pottilogic. Is this what the author of *Alice* is trying to tell us? That the world he is portraying is actually the life we currently live? That *we* are this world?

Should this be the case, I wish to tell you the following (and so conclude): I find it highly irresponsible to call attention to humankind gone astray by means of entertaining little plays like this, irrespective of how amusing they may be. Such issues should be dealt with scientifically, at symposia and political forums. It is not fair of the author, who I presume was also young once, to frighten young people with warnings on how the ground beneath our feet is getting increasingly thinner. How would he have felt if his teachers at school had imposed "ecological thrillers" on him rather than fairy tales, disrupting his sleep by dropping hints that the lifestyle we as parents are leaving to our descendants is not the best? Children should be protected against cruel reality at least up to the age of twenty-five. Afterwards, they can make their own decisions about how to correct the mistakes of their parents.

Therefore, I have no other option but to pass on the following message to every school, college, university, amateur and professional theatre group wishing to stage *Alice in Crazyland* just because it is a good and terribly funny play (I would prefer to say it is not, but I do not want to risk the mockery of my professional colleagues). Be responsible and think twice before putting this subversive play on stage! Even without this, the young are exposed to a whole range of unpleasant ordeals on a daily basis: cuts in hot school meals, peer violence, onerous teachers' demands, lack of money for regular drug-taking and so on. Why burden them with a realistic (if caricatured) image of the world in which they will find themselves after leaving school? The best we can do for our youngsters is to keep them in ignorance about the most pressing problems of our common fate.